The first time I saw the Mighty Mike Quinn, he'd just been declared the undisputed winner of a Saturday-night brawl at my cousin Bennie Chu's Beachside Bar and Grill. He was bigger than life and as blond as a Viking god, bloody but unbowed, with his shirt half torn off, a jagged cut in his palm and one gorgeous green eye nearly swollen shut. As a doctor, I knew he had to be in considerable pain, but you certainly couldn't tell it by looking at him. He sat there on the bar stool, joking with the rest of the patrons, king of all he surveyed. I admit, I might have come across as a little officious and disapproving, but he came on to me while I was patching him up and I had to do *something* to put him in his place. It didn't work. The big lug grabbed me in a hammerlock and kissed me nearly senseless. Then he fainted. I think that's when I began to fall in love with him. Bennie always said I'm a sucker for strays and lost souls.

—Hana Jamieson

MEN at WORK

—MILLIONAIRE'S CLUB —BOARDROOM BOYS —MAGNIFICENT MEN

—TALL, DARK & SMART —DOCTOR, DOCTOR —MEN OF THE WEST

—MEN OF STEEL —MEN IN UNIFORM

MEN at WORK

CANDACE SCHULER

THE MIGHTY QUINN

Harlequin Books

TORONTO • NEW YORK • LONDON
AMSTERDAM • PARIS • SYDNEY • HAMBURG
STOCKHOLM • ATHENS • TOKYO • MILAN
MADRID • WARSAW • BUDAPEST • AUCKLAND

HARLEQUIN BOOKS
225 Duncan Mill Road, Don Mills,
Ontario, Canada M3B 3K9

ISBN 0-373-81046-6

THE MIGHTY QUINN

Dear Reader,

My favorite uncle is a third-generation member of the fire-fighting brotherhood. He's also a heavy rescue expert, which means he does things like tunnel into collapsed buildings to bring out survivors in the event of an earthquake or other disaster. As you might imagine, I've been hearing stories about firefighters most of my life, so I think it was only natural that, eventually, I would write a romance featuring one of these modern-day knights in shining armor as my hero. Mike Quinn, the firefighter in my story, isn't modeled after my uncle—*he's* a happily married man with a newlywed daughter and a son who followed in his footsteps—but Mike's professional exploits are very real. The rescue scene near the end of the book is almost an exact retelling of a rescue my uncle and his team performed after the Mexico City earthquake in 1985, except that they did it fifteen times over.

I hope you enjoy reading *The Mighty Quinn* and that you come away from the story not only believing anew in the power of love but with a fresh appreciation for these unsung heroes of our modern world.

Candace Schulo

To Captain James M. Dellamonica
Salasipuedes Fire District
One of life's real heroes

_____ Prologue _____

HE'D NEVER BEEN AFRAID before. Never even realized he _could_ be afraid. Not him, a man whose
fearlessness was practically legendary; who could
have said, with perfect honesty, that he'd never
felt a moment of real fear in his adult life.

Until now.

But now, like a totally alien presence, the unfa-
miliar emotion was inside him and all around him
at the same time. He could feel it as surely as he
felt the blood oozing down his face from a cut
somewhere over his eyes. It pressed down on him
from outside, more solid and real than the tons of
twisted steel and concrete that held him prisoner;
and from the inside, making his blood run frantically fast and cold, straining his nerves like barbed
wire strung far too tightly, filling his chest with an
unbearable pressure until it was impossible to
take more than one shallow, panting breath after
another.

He could taste the fear, its bitter, metallic flavor
coating his tongue and the back of his throat more
thoroughly than the choking dust that clogged the
dark, tomblike space.

He could smell it, the pungent scent of blood
and bile mixed with the acrid odor of his own
sweat.

He could even hear it. The pounding of his heart

grew louder...and louder...as the unearthly silence of the aftermath gave way to the low moans and terrified, keening cries of those trapped with him.

Shut up, he thought frantically, knowing only too well what effect any sound might have on the precarious stability of the mass above them all. *Just shut up!*

And then he realized that one of the frightened, desperate cries came from deep in his own throat, and that it was his own hot tears of fear, and not just blood, that were trickling down his face and into the matted hair of the small, still body he held in his arms.

Instinct told him he should be doing something for her, that it was his duty to at least check her breathing, or her pulse, or something. But it was useless. *He* was useless. Afraid, and for the first time in his life, utterly, completely useless. Shamed, he pressed his cheek to her hair, closing his eyes tight against the paralyzing fear that gripped him, and began to silently mouth the prayers of his childhood.

down to the water and let the waves wash over
him awhile.

Hana nodded her acceptance of the place. It was
the usual procedure, in fact. Big Louie was too
ornery, even drunk, to tangle with when he
refused to leave or refused to sleep if he'd already
had an awful thirst.

1

THE SMALL WATERFRONT BAR looked like a tornado
had just roared through it. Overturned chairs
were scattered about like a careless child's aban-
doned toys. A table lay on its side, two broken legs
dangling drunkenly. Shards of glass carpeted the
minuscule dance floor in front of the smashed
jukebox. Two men, both lifelong residents of the
island, were trying to get a good grip on a third
man, a full-blooded Polynesian, who was larger
than both of them put together and lay, facedown
and out cold, in front of the wooden bar.

Hana Jamieson sighed. *Another Saturday night in
Paradise*, she thought, her nose wrinkling as the
smell of stale beer and overheated bodies assailed
her. Had it always been like this? Or had her memories of home been softened by time and distance?

She looked down at the unconscious man as his
companions dragged him past her, wondering if
Big Louie was just dead-drunk, as usual, or if
someone bigger than him had contributed a little
muscle to his sorry state. "Is he why I was called
down here?"

Both men glanced up. "No, ma'am," one said
with a sheepish smile. "He ain't hurt, just out cold.
Caught one on the jaw. We're goin' to drag him

down to the water and let the waves wash over him awhile.''

Hana nodded her acceptance of the plan; it was the usual procedure where Big Louie was concerned. ''Don't let him drown,'' she warned. ''And make sure he comes to see me if he has any dizziness or blurred vision.''

''Yes, ma'am.''

She watched them drag the unconscious man out the door by his beefy arms, smiling a little when one of them reached down and cupped Louie's head, as tenderly as a mother would her baby's, lifting it so it wouldn't bounce over the threshold. Then, hefting the weight of her medical bag, she turned toward the bar. She ran her gaze down its length in search of the reason she'd been so rudely awakened on one of the few free Saturday nights she'd had since she returned to Paradise and opened her clinic in the same small house where she'd once helped her father tend to his patients.

There was a knot of men at the far end, noisily offering congratulations—presumably to whoever had cold-cocked Big Louie—and calling for more drinks to celebrate. Stepping gingerly over spilled beer and broken glass, Hana made her way toward them.

''Hey, Bennie,'' she said to the slim Oriental man behind the bar who was busy filling their orders.

The bartender looked up, his scowl changing to a smile when he saw who it was. ''Hey, Hana.'' He slid a beer down the smooth surface of the bar without looking to see if it was caught. He knew it would be; the Saturday-night patrons of Bennie Chu's Beachside Bar and Grill weren't the kind to let good beer go to waste.

"Sorry to call you out so late," he said, wiping his hands on the towel tucked into the apron around his waist. "But I think the Mighty Quinn over there—" he jerked a thumb toward the noisy group still calling for more beer "—is probably gonna need stitches. Big Louie got in a good lick or two before he went down."

"Mighty Quinn?" Hana queried. Paradise was a small island in a chain of small islands in the South Pacific; she'd grown up on its confines, was related to half of its inhabitants, and knew most of the rest by their first names, but the name Quinn— Mighty or otherwise—didn't ring any bells.

"He's new in Paradise," Bennie said. "Real moniker's Mike Quinn. Or so he says. One of those knotheads down there tacked on the 'Mighty' after he flattened Big Louie."

Hana made a moue of distaste. "One of the off-island construction workers from the hotel?" she asked.

Bennie shook his head as he sent another beer sailing down the bar in answer to a noisy summons. "Just a drifter. Dropped anchor a couple of weeks ago over in John's Cove." A wide appreciative smile split his face for a second, narrowing his almond-shaped eyes to mere slits. "Prettiest little sloop you ever saw. 'Bout twenty-five feet and slick as spit."

Hana nodded but her frown didn't fade. She'd heard about the beautiful sloop in John's Cove— news traveled fast in Paradise—but in her book drifters ranked only slightly above the construction workers who'd been imported from off-island to put a high-rise hotel complex on Paradise's southernmost shore. Construction workers, drifters, tourists, even—they all spelled trouble for Paradise, one way or another. Still, she decided, as a drifter, at least he wasn't tearing up her home in the name of progress, so she guessed she could tend his wounds. Besides, it was part of the Hippocratic oath.

"Which one is he?"

"Big blond dude with his pretty face all bashed up. You can't miss him."

Hana glanced down toward the group at the end of the bar. All she saw were a half-dozen or so broad male backs. She knew the owners of most of those backs, true, and they were basically good guys. But they were all bigger than her, and they were drinking. Not good odds for a woman at the best of times, let alone when combined with all the testosterone-fueled aggression undoubtedly racing through their bodies after witnessing a bar brawl.

I should have taken the time to change my clothes, she thought, glancing down at her bare legs, *and hung a stethoscope around my neck.* But she'd been asleep in the hammock on the lanai behind her clinic when the call came, and she hadn't taken the time to do anything more than shove her feet into a pair of thongs and grab her medical bag.

"I've still got that baseball bat under the bar," Bennie said, noting her hesitation. "And there's a handgun in the cash register."

Hana gave him a slight nod and a smile and,

taking a deep breath, moved on down the bar. She tapped the nearest man on the shoulder. "Excuse me." The man glanced around, moving aside when he saw who it was. Relieved, Hana gave him a quick frown, letting him know his mother was going to find out where he'd spent his Saturday night, and tapped another broad back. "Excuse me, please. I need to get through."

"Hey, let the doctor through, will ya?" the young man she'd frowned at said helpfully, obviously trying to redeem himself. "She needs to take a look at Quinn's hand. Shove over."

There was some jostling, and then the group parted, giving Hana her first view of her patient. One look confirmed what she already knew. The drifter was Trouble. As big and blond as a Viking, with the tattered remains of a faded blue chambray shirt hanging open over a wide, tanned, golden-haired chest and a cocky, renegade grin quirking up one corner of his mouth, he was the stuff of a thousand female fantasies and a hundred male nightmares. Three days' worth of stubble and a rapidly swelling eye only added to his rugged appeal.

And she was sure he knew it.

He sat half perched on a barstool, his elbow bent, his left hand resting, palm up, on the scratched surface of the bar, his fingers loosely curled around a blood-spattered towel. There was a beer in his other hand, which was balanced on the lush, sarong-clad hip of the exotic Eurasian woman standing in the curve of his arm. She was cooing and fussing over him, using a bar towel dipped in bourbon to dab at the cut over his swollen eye. He accepted her ministrations with the lazy nonchalance of a spoiled prince, as if feminine attention and concern were his by divine right.

The Mighty Quinn, indeed, Hana thought dryly. *First-class macho jerk was more like it.* "Excuse me," she said again, more loudly. Her tone dripped disapproval.

He looked up then, straight into her eyes. Hana stared into a green as pale and clear as the water in the shallows of John's Cove for a scant second longer than was comfortable. She looked away first.

Arrogant bastard, she thought, instantly and instinctively on her guard. There was something definitely predatory in his expression.

Self-righteous prig, he thought, instantly offended by the condemnation in her wide, dark eyes.

She set her medical bag on the bar with an authoritative thump and motioned toward the bloody rag in his hand in a deliberate attempt to set the boundaries between them. "I'll need a little space," she said as steadily as she could.

"What?" The woman in Quinn's loose embrace turned around, her eyes narrowing at the sight of another woman apparently trying to move in on what she considered was hers. "Who are you?"

"I'm a doctor," Hana said evenly, matching the woman stare for stare, wondering who she was. A woman who was paid by the hour, certainly, but not from the island; abruptly Hana realized the rumors she'd heard about the hotel developers importing professional "companions" for the construction crews must be true.

"You don't look like any doctor to me," the woman challenged, her gaze on Hana's orange tank top and the long black braid hanging over her shoulder. She cast a coy, sideways glance at Quinn. "She look like a doctor to you, honey?"

"She is, too, a doctor," said the young man who had cleared Hana's way before "honey" could answer. "In fact, she's the only doctor in Paradise." There was more than a touch of civic pride in his voice.

"Well, la-de-da." The woman lifted a bare shoulder. "You can just take yourself outta here, doctor or no," she said to Hana as she turned back into Quinn's embrace and resumed dabbing at the cut over his eye. "We don't need you. Do we, honey?" she cooed.

"You may not need her," Quinn said, sending a suggestive, speculative glance toward Hana as he spoke, "but I do." He removed his arm from around the woman's waist and put his beer down on the bar, then set her away from him, smacking her on the bottom as he did so. "Go on, Angel, get the hell out of the way so the doctor can attend—" he placed a subtle, mocking emphasis on the word "—to me."

"Well, I never—" the woman began huffily.

Quinn gave her a lazy smile. "Sure you have, honey. And you will again. Later." He wrapped his uninjured hand around the back of her neck and pulled her close for a long, thorough kiss. Angel acquiesced immediately, melting against him and kissing him back with all the professional expertise she possessed.

The men hooted and hollered, offering encouragement.

Hana flushed, feeling suddenly, uncomfortably warm. She'd never seen a kiss so blatantly carnal outside the confines of a movie theater.

"Be a good girl, now," Quinn said when he lifted his mouth from Angel's. "And get lost." He picked up one of the bills on the bar and tucked it into her cleavage. "I'll see you later."

The woman turned and, after flashing a triumphant little smile at Hana, strolled toward the door with a deliberately sensual stride, aware that every man in the place was watching her. She paused in the doorway, glanced over her bare shoulder, and blew a kiss. The men hooted again as Quinn made a show of pretending to catch it in his fist and blow it back. Despite his show of dubious gallantry, it was obvious that the minute she was out of sight, she was also out of mind. Quinn immediately turned his gaze—still suggestive, still speculative—to Hana. The eyebrow over his unswollen eye quirked upward. "Well, Doc?"

Hana responded instinctively to the challenge. "If you gentlemen—" the disparagement in the slight inflection she gave the word was deliberate "—could give me a little room?" she said, her level gaze touching each man in turn. They slunk away without a word, even the ones she didn't know, like naughty little boys chastised by Mother. Her unruly audience neatly dispensed with, Hana turned briskly and, without meeting her patient's eyes, lifted the bloody towel from Quinn's hand.

It was a nasty wound—a deep, jagged line cutting diagonally across his palm, already clotting in some places, still oozing blood in others.

"What did you do?" she asked calmly, showing none of her natural revulsion to the effects of violence. "Try to take a broken beer bottle away from Big Louie with your bare hands?"

"It was better than taking it in the face."

"You could have tried walking away from it," she suggested.

"No," he said flatly. "I couldn't."

At the change in his voice, from lazy nonchalance to deadly seriousness, she looked up quickly. "Why—"

"Defending a lady's honor, don't ya know," he said, interrupting whatever question she'd been about to ask. The insouciance was back in his voice, the lazy challenge evident in his expression, making her think she'd imagined the change.

A lady's honor, my eye, she thought, shaking her head in disgust at the things men did in the name of lust.

"You don't approve?"

"It's none of my business," Hana replied stiffly, reaching into her case for her instruments.

"That's right," Quinn agreed, just to needle her. "It isn't."

Hana refused to rise to the bait, concentrating instead on laying out the instruments she'd need, trying to pretend her patient was just like any other patient she'd ever attended to. She had to be calm, cool and collected to do her job with any degree of efficiency and, for the first time since her internship, she was finding that particularly hard to do. She was absolutely positive it was all his fault, despite the fact that he wasn't actually doing anything she could object to.

The man who was taking perverse and quite deliberate pleasure in making Hana's life difficult at the moment sat, silent and assessing, as he watched her methodically prepare to cause more pain to his already aching body. As Angel had said, she didn't look much like a doctor, not in the baggy white shorts, orange tank top and rubber thongs she was wearing. And no doctor he'd ever seen had such long, tanned legs. She didn't smell the least bit medicinal, either. Her scent reminded him more of suntan lotion and salt water than hospitals and doctors' offices. The thick black braid hanging over her shoulder made him think of beaches, too, and got him to wondering what her hair would look like hanging, unbraided and wet with seawater, down her naked back.

No, she didn't look like his idea of a doctor at all.

Feeling suddenly magnanimous, Quinn decided he didn't mind. Certainly not the way she looked. Nor the disapproving, holier-than-thou way she acted, either. He'd had his fill of medical types over the past year or so, but watching her little round breasts move under the cotton knit of her top as she laid out her instruments went a long way toward canceling out his annoyance over her attitude. Besides, it gave him something to think about other than the throbbing pain in his right hand. And he really needed something else to think about just then; despite the alcohol he'd consumed, parts of him were hurting like a son of a bitch.

"So, Doc," he said, his voice whisper-rough and as intimate as sin, "this gonna hurt?"

Not nearly as much as it should, Hana thought, trying desperately to ignore his nearness as she filled a hypodermic syringe with painkilling medication. But somebody as big as the Mighty Mike Quinn was darned hard to ignore. On top of which, he had incredible gall.

Or, she decided, *incredible stamina.*

How many other men in his condition—bleeding from the jagged cut in the palm of his hand as well as from the lesser wound above his swollen eye, his shirt torn and blood-spattered, and stinking of sweat, beer and cheap perfume—would have the energy, let alone the audacity, to come on to her? She frowned, flicking the barrel of the hypo with her finger with more force than necessary to settle its contents.

Drunks!

The only way to deal with one was to do what had to be done as quickly and with as little conversation as possible and then beat a path to the nearest door, because there was no telling what a drunk would do. Especially the big, macho ones who thought liquor turned them into Prince Charming.

She turned toward him with the filled hypodermic in her right hand, needle carefully tilted upward. "Are you allergic to anything I should know about?"

"Just cold-hearted women."

Hana pretended she hadn't heard that. "Penicillin? Painkillers?"

He shook his head.

"Straighten your fingers a bit," she ordered, motioning with the hand that held the needle. "I need to see what I'm doing."

"Doc?" His uninjured hand curled around her wrist, halting further movement. "I'm *real* sensitive to pain."

Hana lifted her lashes and looked directly at him. The disdainful expression in her dark brown eyes collided with the leering challenge in his one open green one. "You should have thought of that sooner," she said and tried to shake him off.

His grip tightened fractionally, not enough to hurt but enough to hold. "Sooner?"

"Before you started this—" an almost-imperceptible movement of her head encompassed the trashed bar "—brawl."

"Who says I started it?" he demanded, his irritation returning at the disapproving look on her face. Who the hell was she to judge him, anyway?

Hana raised a delicate, disdainful eyebrow. "Didn't you?"

"Yeah," he lied, giving her his most charming smirk, his unswollen eye sweeping the bar with the puffed-up pride of a precocious four-year-old. "I did start it." His gaze came back to hers. "But, like I said, I had a good reason. Didn't I, Bennie?" he said, raising his voice slightly in order to be heard by the bartender, who was sweeping up broken glass. His gaze—sly, knowing, intensely personal—never left Hana's.

"Didn't you what?" Bennie asked in a bored voice.

"Have a good reason for starting this—" his slight pause perfectly imitated hers "—brawl."

Bennie gave a muffled snort. "If you call fighting over a used piece of ta—" His gaze flickered over Hana. "Over a woman a good reason."

"I do," Quinn affirmed. "In fact, I consider it an honor to fight for the favors of a lady." His voice dropped back to an intimate whisper. "I'd fight for your—" he let his gaze drop down to Hana's breasts and back "—favors any time, Doc." He pulled her closer by the wrist he still held, so close that his bourbon-and-beer-scented breath fanned against her cheek with each soft, suggestive word. "Whaddaya say, Doc? Would you like to watch me fight for the honor of taking you to bed?"

Hana stiffened but stood her ground. "What I'd *like*," she said steadily, even though her heart was pounding, "is for you to try to act like a civilized human being and let me do my job."

"Civilized, hmm?" He pretended to consider that. "That's funny. My women usually like it more when I'm—" he moved another fraction of an inch closer, so close that his lips were practically touching hers "—uncivilized."

Hana's head snapped back, out of range of his lips. "How fortunate for you that your women are so easily pleased," she said coldly, giving him stare for stare. "And how fortunate for me that I'm not one of them."

Anger surged through him at her scathing defiance. "We could fix that," he said. And then, ignoring both her gasp of outrage and the hypodermic in her hand, he let go of her wrist, wrapped his arm around her waist, yanked her to him and covered her mouth with his.

Every nerve in Hana's body signaled red alert. She went rigid, instinctively arching her back to put as much distance between their bodies as possible. She pushed against the hard wall of his chest with her forearms, pressing her lips tightly together to repel the advance of his tongue. But it was no use. She was surrounded by him, overwhelmingly aware of the surprising softness of his lips, of the scrape of his stubbled jaw against the sensitive skin around her mouth, of the strangely tender strength of the one arm that held her fast—and of the hypodermic needle she still held, very carefully, in her right hand.

If I had any sense, I'd stab him with it, she thought furiously.

And then he leaned into her heavily, overpowering her with his size and weight, frightening her in a way she'd never been frightened before. She dropped the needle and wrapped her arms around his waist, suddenly realizing that she was the one doing the holding instead of the one being held.

The Mighty Quinn had fainted.

2

"HOLD HIM RIGHT HERE for a second, Bennie," Hana said, letting go of her patient long enough to flip on the lights and set her medical bag on the stand next to the one and only examining table in her clinic. She hurried back to the two men braced against the doorjamb and eased herself under Quinn's arm. "Okay, easy now," she instructed, wedging her shoulder firmly into his armpit to take as much of his weight as possible from Bennie's slender frame. She slipped her other hand around Quinn's lean torso, curling her fingers in the waistband of his jeans to get a firm grip in case he blacked out again—which he'd already done twice between the bar and her clinic. "We don't want to jostle him around any more than we have to."

Bennie gave her a sour look from under lowered brows, unable to lift his head more than a few inches because of the heavy arm draped around his neck. "How many times have I helped you drag drunks in here?"

Hana flashed him an apologetic smile. "Too many," she said, the smile fading as she thought of just how many times he'd helped her with one particular drunk. Quinn stumbled against her, letting out a grunt of pain, and the unsettling memory fled in the face of more immediate problems. She shifted her arm around his narrow waist, getting a better grip. "But he's not just drunk, he's hurt."

"'Nother kiss, sweetheart," Quinn mumbled. His warm breath fanned the side of her face as he nuzzled her cheek in search of her mouth.

"Not all that drunk, apparently," Bennie commented dryly as Hana tilted her head to avoid Quinn's seeking lips.

"Don' be shy, honey," Quinn coaxed. Undeterred by her evasive action, he nibbled at her neck as they shuffled and weaved toward the bamboo screens that shielded the examining table. The hand hanging over her shoulder groped for her breast, ending up tangled in her long black braid instead. "No need to be shy with ol' Quinn," he said, trying to free his fingers from the silky strands of her hair.

Hana clamped her hand over his to curtail any further exploration. "Let's get him up on the examining table," she said to Bennie, managing to sound calm and cool despite the way her pulse had begun to jump. "No..." She paused in momentary indecision. The examining table would make it easier on her but not, in this instance, on her patient. "Let's put him on one of the beds instead. That way, we won't have to move him again after I've patched him up."

Bennie nodded and they changed direction, heading around the bamboo-and-fabric divider that separated Hana's examining room from the three beds that made up her hospital ward. Easing out from under his burden, Bennie moved around to the opposite side of the bed to assist the doctor in getting her patient up on it. He reached across the narrow bed, taking hold of the back of Quinn's jeans. Hana disentangled her braid from Quinn's hand and tossed it back over her shoulder where it would be out of harm's way. "Ready?" she asked.

"Ready, willin' an' able," Quinn said, attempting a leering wink with his one good eye.

"Okay." Hana shifted her grip. "And...lift."

Hana pushed. Bennie pulled. All three of them grunted with the effort.

"Easy there, honey," Quinn complained as he fell back on the bed. He managed, as he fell, to drag Hana down on top of him. "No need to be so rou—" His arms went lax around her.

"Blacked out again," Bennie said.

"No kidding," Hana mumbled into the hair-dusted dampness of Quinn's wide chest. She could smell the freshness of sea air and the faint scent of the same coconut suntan lotion she used beneath the heavy, musky fragrance of the perfume favored by the woman he'd recently gotten himself beaten up over. Telling herself not to breathe too deeply, Hana moved her hand from the middle of his chest and, pressing her palm against the mattress, pushed herself upright. Quinn's hand fell away from her shoulder, sliding down her arm to lie, curled inward and looking utterly defenseless, against the stark white of the hospital sheets. It was all Hana could do not to pick it up and cradle it in both of hers.

"Let's get him undressed," she said briskly, to cover the sudden, unexpected rush of tenderness. Drunks and brawlers didn't deserve any special tenderness, she told herself sternly as she reached for the waistband of his low-slung jeans. She'd flicked open half the buttons on his fly before realizing he wore no underwear beneath the faded denim. Her hands checked in midmotion. *He'll be naked*, she thought, reacting like a schoolgirl who'd never seen an unclothed man instead of a doctor who was fully conversant with the intimate workings of the male body.

"Anything wrong?" Bennie asked.

Hana grabbed a sheet from the pile stored in the open shelves between the beds and flicked it over her patient's lower body, then moved to his feet as if that were what she'd intended to do all along. "Shoes first," she said, tugging the sandy, salt-spotted deck shoes off his heels.

Leaving Bennie to deal with the removal of Quinn's jeans under the cover of the sheet, Hana moved up her patient's torso and peeled back the halves of his bloodied chambray shirt. Slipping her arm under him, she lifted his shoulder so she could slide the tattered garment off. The dark, purplish bruise marring the entire left side of his lean rib-cage stopped her.

"Oh, Lord," she breathed as she gently lowered him back to the bed.

He could have broken ribs or a punctured lung, she thought, and they'd manhandled him into and out of her old rattletrap of a van, jostled him over the rutted, gravel roads between Bennie's bar and her clinic, dragged him inside and dropped him on a bed. And then she'd fallen on him! No wonder he'd passed out again.

"Big Louie hit him with a chair," Bennie said, watching as she delicately probed the ugly bruise.

Quinn moaned.

Hana's fingers stilled, going from inquisitive to comforting in a heartbeat. Unconsciously she flattened her palm, smoothing it over the bruised area in a gentling motion. Almost instantly, Quinn quieted.

"I'm going to cut his shirt off," she decided, loath to cause him any more pain. "Watch him while I get my bag."

Though she was only gone a few minutes—just long enough to wash her hands, slip into her lab coat and retrieve her bag—Quinn was fretting when she returned to his bedside. His head was moving restlessly, his broad shoulders twitching under Bennie's restraining hands as he hovered in the gray area between painful consciousness and blessed, pain-free unconsciousness.

"Can't move," he murmured. "So dark. Can't move…can't… Holding me down."

Hana put down her bag and bent over him. "It's okay," she said, as gently as if she were speaking to a frightened child. "It's only Bennie, making sure you don't roll off the bed."

"Quiet!" He barked out the command in an anguished whisper. "Be quiet!"

Hana waved Bennie away and reached out, placing her hands on Quinn's shoulders. "Yes, be quiet," she whispered. "We'll all be quiet." She stroked his shoulders and down his arms, gentling and soothing him. "Hush, now, and lie still while I get this shirt off you."

He turned his head toward the sound of her

voice, mumbling something unintelligible and urgent. She sensed more than heard the rising inflection that made it a question.

"Yes." She answered in the affirmative in an instinctive effort to comfort and calm him. "Yes. But lie still now and be quiet." She moved one hand to his bare chest, still using the soft, stroking touches women have always used to soothe the ailing and infirm. "Everything will be all right. You're going to be just fine."

Quinn sighed, contented, and slipped completely under again.

Hana's gaze sought Bennie's for a brief moment. "Let's get him patched up before he comes to."

She cut away his shirt, gently pulling it from under him, and dropped it to the floor. She cleaned his chest and ribs with warm, antiseptic-laced water and a soft cloth, her skilled fingers gently searching for signs of a break. Without an X-ray machine it was impossible to know for sure, of course, but she didn't have an X-ray machine. The best she could do was feel for any obvious breaks, listen for the rattles or raspy breathing that would indicate a punctured lung and, finding neither, tape him up as tightly as possible to forestall any further injury. Taping wouldn't hurt him if nothing was broken; not taping could conceivably kill him if something was.

That done, she cleaned his open wounds with sterile gauze and more antiseptic, stitched his hand, then went ahead and took a couple of stitches in the small cut over his eye to minimize potential scarring. There was nothing modern medicine could do for the swelling bruise that puffed up around his eye, but ancient medical practices could probably bring the swelling down enough so he could open his eye tomorrow, as well as keep him from developing a real shiner.

"You can't tell me they taught you *that* in medical school," Bennie said as he watched her dip a small pair of tongs into a jar containing what looked like small, black slugs.

"As a matter of fact, they did." She placed a small slug on the purple area just below the cut above Quinn's eye. "I did my residency under a doctor who did a lot of plastic surgery," she said, positioning another slug on the bone beneath the eye socket, where the worst swelling was. "He's been using leeches for the last several years, especially with face-lifts and eyelid tucks. They help reduce the bruising by leeching out the blood that causes it. *If* they're applied early enough." She set the jar aside. "We'll just have to wait and see how well they work on the Mighty Quinn, here."

"Don't they hurt him?" Bennie's expression, as he watched the leeches fill with blood, was one of fascinated disgust.

"You've seen *The African Queen* too many times," Hana said, flashing him an amused look from behind the hypodermic she was filling. "They look and feel kind of yucky but they don't hurt. They emit a chemical—we don't know exactly what—that penetrates through the skin and inhibits clotting so they can feed." She swabbed Quinn's arm with alcohol and administered the tetanus booster she'd prepared. "Leeches have been used very successfully in the reattachment of limbs, too," she went on, her eyes on her patient as she delicately lifted his lids to check for pupil response with her ophthalmoscope. It was normal, assuring her that he hadn't suffered a concussion along with his other injuries. "Like when a finger has been cut off," she said, straightening to look at Bennie across the width of the bed. "Leeches are placed along the suture line to keep the blood from clotting and cutting off the flow to the reattachment. And when they're full, they just fall off." Using her small tongs, she picked up the leech that had detached itself and rolled onto Quinn's pillow. "See?" She held it up for Bennie's inspection. It was big and fat now, engorged with the blood that would have resulted in a black eye.

"Disgusting," Bennie said.

"Very," she agreed, dropping it into an empty jar. "But useful." She removed the second sated leech, dropping it into the jar with the first, and screwed down the lid.

She then took another set of blood-pressure and pulse readings, rechecked the cuts on both his forehead and hand, and finally, applied light sterile dressings to both wounds. By the time she was satisfied she'd done all she could do, her patient was beginning to resurface through the layers of unconsciousness, his hard muscles flexing uneasily beneath her ministrations.

Hana sighed and straightened, the fingers of one hand absently stroking his arm soothingly, her other hand pressing against the small of her back to relieve the ache caused by bending over the bed for so long. "That's all we can do for him now," she said to Bennie, who'd served as her more-than-capable assistant through the entire procedure. Her smile was wan with fatigue. "You've been a rock."

"You gonna be all right?"

"A good night's sleep and I'll be fine." She smoothed the edge of the surgical tape around Quinn's torso, making sure the ends were secure.

"Can you do that and watch him at the same time?"

"What?" She lifted her gaze from her patient to Bennie. "Sleep?"

Bennie nodded.

"Sure." She motioned toward the adjoining bed. "I'll just sack out there so I'll be available in case he needs anything. It's not as if I haven't done it a hundred times before," she added before Bennie could object to the plan. "We won't have a nurse on the weekends until Reiko comes back." She sighed. "*If* she comes back."

Not that Hana would have blamed the young woman if she didn't return to Paradise when she graduated from nursing school; there wasn't a whole lot of opportunity for career advancement on the tiny island.

"She'll come back," Bennie said with the conviction of a close relative; the young woman in question was one of his many cousins, just as Hana was, only much less distant. "Reiko loves Paradise as much as you do."

"I'm counting on that." Hana looked down at her patient as she spoke, reaching out to check the bandage covering the cut over his eye. His forehead was warmer than she liked. Frowning, she touched his cheek. "I should probably try to get a couple of aspirin into him," she said as she shifted her hand back to his forehead.

Still mostly unconscious, Quinn turned into her touch, snuggling his forehead into her palm with a soft "Mmm" of pleasure. Hana smiled and smoothed the heavy, sun-streaked strands of his hair back with a lingering caress.

"Hana?" Bennie said.

"Hmm?" she murmured, her brow furrowing as she continued to look down at her patient. Penicillin would be better at helping him fight off a possible infection and the accompanying fever, she thought, still stroking his head, but her supply of penicillin was low right now, as it nearly always was, and she hated to use it if she didn't have to. Aspirin would do for now, she decided. If stronger measures were called for later, she would deal with it later. But she didn't think stronger measures would be called for; even unconscious, the Mighty Mike Quinn looked more than robust enough to overcome any infection induced by the injuries he'd sustained.

His torso was hard and wedge-shaped beneath the surgical tape—impressively wide through the chest, and narrow and washboard-firm through the waist and hips. His bare arms and shoulders were a deep golden brown against the white sheets and bandages, roped with smooth muscles that looked powerful even in repose. His face was a Viking maiden's dream: a strong blade of a nose, a square, uncompromising chin, a jaw and cheekbones of chisel-sharp purity despite the swollen bruise and unshaven stubble. He had the mouth of a fallen angel. She touched the well-defined bow of his upper lip with a soft fingertip, wondering how something so unabashedly male and sexy could also convey more than a hint of little-boy sweetness and vulnerability.

"Hana?" Bennie said again.

Hana looked up, surprised to see him still hovering on the opposite side of the bed. "Why don't you go on home," she suggested, hastily stuffing her hands into the pockets of her lab coat. "I can handle it from here. Go on," she urged, her gaze already drifting back down to her patient's face. "You must be beat."

"You sure you can handle him?"

No, I'm not sure at all. The thought came out of nowhere, surprising her with its vehemence. She put it down to tiredness. "He's unconscious," she said to Bennie. "I'd be a poor excuse for a doctor if I couldn't handle him in this condition, now wouldn't I?"

SHE WAS AWAKENED a few hours later by the sound of someone whimpering like a trapped animal. Conditioned by the grueling internship meted out to all doctor wannabees, she was instantly alert and fully aware of where she was and what she was supposed to be doing.

Her patient was in pain.

She swung her feet over the side of the narrow bed and reached him in two steps. Her aim unerring even in the dark, she palmed his cheek to feel for fever. He was warm but not alarmingly so, indicating that the aspirin she'd given him earlier had done its work. What was alarming, however, was the dampness of his skin and the lank wet hair lying on his forehead; he was sweating as if he'd just run a marathon. Worse, his breathing was labored and raspy.

His ribs? she wondered, running her hands down his sides to check the bandages. Her eyes had adjusted to the dim light of the half-moon shining in through the window, but it was her acute sense of touch more than sight that assured her the tape wound around his ribs was still securely in place. Her fingers feathered over his torso, anyway, checking for any abnormalities under the tight bindings.

He caught her exploring hand in his, crushing it against his chest. "Can't breathe," he said, even though his breath was bellowing in and out of his lungs. "Can't breathe. No air." His voice was an anguished whisper. "Dark. So dark. Pressing out all the air."

"It's all right," Hana whispered, trying to work her hand from his grasp so she could help him. If he was having trouble breathing, something was definitely wrong, taping or no taping. "Just let me turn on the light so I can—"

His fingers tightened painfully. "Don't go," he pleaded. "Don't leave me in the dark."

"Just for a minute." She managed to slip her fingers out of his hand. "Just let me—"

He grabbed her wrist and held on tightly. *"Don't leave me alone!"*

It was a primal cry of terror and Hana responded to it on the same primal level. Without stopping to think about what she was doing, she sank down onto the edge of the bed and took him into her arms.

He was shaking and sweating like a child in the throes of a terrifying nightmare and, with a profound sense of relief, Hana realized that that's exactly what it was. He wasn't suffering from any physical pain—at least, not at the moment—he was having a nightmare. She bent lower and cradled his head to her breast, instinctively offering the comfort and succor he needed far more than any medical attention she could give him. "I'm right here," she murmured. "Hana's right here."

"Don't leave," he said again, wrapping his arms around her as if to make sure she wouldn't.

Hana lifted her legs onto the bed, allowing herself to be drawn down beside him. "No, I won't leave." She stroked his damp hair back from his forehead. "I won't leave."

Her voice reassured him, her touch calmed him and, between one breath and the next, he fell back into a deep, seemingly dreamless sleep with his face snuggled into her breasts and his arms hard around her.

Hana lay quietly in his embrace, still stroking his head. Her last thought before drifting off into sleep herself was to wonder what on earth could so terrify a man like Mike Quinn that he would cry out like a child afraid of the dark.

HE WOKE AGAIN IN THE SOFT gray light that precedes dawn, but quietly this time, coming slowly and naturally into full awareness. His aching body told him he'd been in a fight. Various individual pains pinpointed the exact location of specific injuries, allowing him to catalog the swollen eye and the bruised ribs as nothing new and, therefore, not worth worrying about. The dull, throbbing pain in his left hand caused him a moment's concern until a few careful, flexing movements told him it had been stitched and bandaged and, more important, was still fully functional. He relaxed and set his mind to the task of figuring out *why* he'd been in a fight.

He'd been drinking, of course. Not enough to be truly drunk, but near enough to it to make any traffic cop want to argue the point, and more than enough to make him wish for the restorative effects of a couple of extra-strength aspirin and a bracing shower. There'd been a woman involved—Angie or Angel something—and some guy as big as a mountain who'd tried to cut him in half with a chair.

Little by little, it all came back to him until he recalled, quite clearly, exactly where and why the fight had been fought. He'd won—that much was a given because he always won any fight he got into—but he seemed to remember watching the woman he'd fought over—Angel, he was sure of it now—walk out the door of Bennie's Beachside Bar and Grill all by her lonesome.

So who was the warm, sweet bundle of femininity he was snuggled up to?

Quinn lifted his head, reluctantly unsnuggling his cheek from the soft breast where it lay, and peered up into the face of the woman who held him in her arms while she slept. Definitely not Angel. Her skin was smooth and honey-gold, the faint flush on her cheeks and the inky blackness of her brows and lashes achieved, not by the heavy application of the various cosmetics favored by most ladies of the evening, but by the more subtle hand of Mother Nature. Instead of a headful of artful curls spread over the pillow, a single long braid, black as midnight and nearly as thick as his wrist, lay over her shoulder. The end had come unbound and was fanned out over the bright orange of her tank top, partially obscuring the breast on which his cheek had been resting. And her breasts, though sinfully soft and infinitely comforting, weren't the pillowy D-cups Angel had pressed against him in the bar. They were as small and sweet as summer peaches, each one barely a handful for a man with paws as big as his.

"Well, I'll be damned," Mike Quinn murmured. "It's the lady doc."

3

HOW IN THE HELL had he ended up in her bed?

He remembered their eyes meeting in the bar and the instant electricity and elemental man-woman wariness that had sparked to life between them. He remembered admiring her soft, slender curves while they sparred with each other. He remembered—vaguely—a ride in a rattletrap old van with her snuggled up to his side. He had a shadowy recollection of her leaning over him and touching him, rubbing her soft, cool hands over his arms and chest while she crooned sweet, loving words. He even remembered himself, whispering all the right sweet-nothings in return and fumbling for her breast—an unforgivable lapse of technique he blamed on the unfortunate combination of pain and alcohol—as they fell onto the bed.

But he also remembered her disapproving, nose-in-the-air attitude in the bar and his deliberate rudeness in response. Which, of course, had only increased her disapproval. So what had changed her mind about him? What had induced her to so far forget her disapproval as to invite him into her bed? And then he remembered the kiss. An utterly masculine, supremely self-satisfied grin spread over his face.

Well, whaddaya know, he thought. *One kiss and the self-righteous lady doctor turns into a warm-blooded woman.* And, after ministering to his physical injuries with her medical skills, she'd obviously been charmed by his wounded-warrior routine into soothing his troubled soul with the delights of her body. *Damn, I'm good,* he congratulated himself, wishing he could remember exactly what the delights of her body entailed.

But his memory had become hazy and uncooperative somewhere between falling onto the bed with her and the present. He had the niggling, uneasy feeling it might have been because what had happened between them wasn't worth remembering. He could only assume he'd been hurried and—as much as he hated to admit it—probably clumsy in his lovemaking of the night before. If, in fact, there'd actually *been* any real lovemaking. Given the state of her dress and the fact that she was on top of the sheet while he was under it, it was doubtful. Still, he thought, she hadn't kicked him out of her bed, so, whatever had happened, it probably hadn't been all that bad.

And he could certainly make it better.

He moved the tail of her braid out of his way with careful fingers and laid his head back down on the soft, inviting cushion of her firm little breasts. Wrapping his arms more securely around her, he gathered her slim, bed-warmed body more fully into his embrace.

She stirred sleepily, crooning something unintelligible as she cuddled him closer and stroked his head.

Grinning like a demented Cheshire cat, Quinn

nudged down the edge of her orange top with his chin and took the tip of her bare breast into his mouth.

Her stroking fingers paused, then curled into his hair and pulled him closer, as if asking for more.

Eager to oblige her, Quinn opened his lips wider and gently took more of her breast into his mouth.

She sighed and arched into the caress.

He drew back and blew on her pebbled nipple, knowing the coolness after the warmth of his mouth would make the sensation even more intense.

She shivered and tugged on his head.

Quinn resisted the pull of her guiding hands and, mindful of his bruised ribs, levered himself up her body to look into her face. She was still asleep, or as close to it as to make no difference. And that wasn't nearly good enough. Despite whatever had or had not happened the previous night, he preferred both parties involved be fully awake and aware; it was more fun that way.

"Wake up," he whispered and brushed his mouth across hers.

Her lips parted and her hands tightened in his hair.

"None of that now," he said, his voice rich with satisfaction and anticipation. If she responded this passionately asleep, he thought, how much more passionately would she respond when she knew what, and who, she was responding to? Just the thought of what he'd missed made him regret the night before even more than he already did.

"Come on, honey, wake up and look at me. Oh, all right," he agreed when her eyes refused to open and her chin lifted invitingly. "Just one more."

Intending only to brush another teasing kiss across her lips, he bent his head the fraction of an inch required and touched his mouth to hers. But her taste was so sweet, so warm, so exactly what he seemed to need, that he couldn't stop himself from taking it deeper. He slanted his head to increase the pressure and plunged his tongue between her parted lips. His hand moved downward at the same time and he palmed her bare breast, capturing the nipple he'd teased to hardness with his mouth between his thumb and forefinger.

He felt awareness zing through her as she came completely awake. Her body jerked in startled reaction and her hands moved from his head to his shoulders. Her fingers curled, clutching at him, then flared, pressing hard. Making wild little noises in her throat, she writhed beneath him. Thinking only that passion was making her squirm in uncontrollable lust, Quinn tightened his arms around her to keep her from falling off the bed and, not coincidentally, to protect his ribs. Her movements intensified as he pulled her more fully under him and, with a heave of her body and a muffled moan, she tore her mouth free of his.

"What the *hell* do you think—" Hana began, but words failed her. She could only stare, wide-eyed and disbelieving, at the beautiful, battle-scarred Viking looming over her, looking at her as if she were his by right of conquest. She tried very hard not to be thrilled by it, deliberately concentrating on the stale smell of beer and bourbon on his breath instead; it carried enough painful memories to counteract the feel of his body against hers.

Quinn returned her stare, entranced. She was breathing in short gasps, her lips parted, the soft little breast—just *exactly* a handful—cupped in his hand rising and falling with each breath. Her smooth, tanned cheeks were flushed with the wild roses of passion. Her eyes were wide with the wonder of it, the dilated pupils making them look almost black in the soft light of dawn. Her sweet, delectable mouth was dewy from his kiss.

Beautiful, he thought, and lowered his head to kiss her again.

"No." Hana shoved at his shoulder, panicked at both the intent she saw in his eyes and her own surprising urge to give in to what she saw. "Wait just a—"

"I can't wait," Quinn said, his voice gone all husky and gruff. It had been a game until now—a meaningless, inconsequential game with sweet release as the prize for both of them—but, suddenly, it was something more. He needed her. Desperately. *This must have been the way it was last night,* he reflected with sudden insight. *Last night I must have needed her like this.* And she had been there, sweet and warm and strangely comforting, giving him what he needed, the way she would give him what he needed now. "I'll slow down next time," he murmured against her mouth. "I'll make it so good for you next time, you'll—"

"There won't be a next time," Hana said, frantically trying to push him away. Or was she? Her hands were still braced on his shoulders, but was she pushing as hard as she could? Or at all? And was she making it as difficult for his lips to find hers as it should be? She twisted her head on the pillow and pushed harder, redoubling her efforts at resisting him. "There won't be a next time," she said again, more forcefully. "There wasn't even a *last* time."

"And I'm sorry about that," Quinn said. "Really—" denied her mouth, his lips went on a hurried journey down the arched line of her throat "—really—" they brushed over the upper curve of her exposed breast "—sorry," he finished and closed his lips over her nipple.

Hana gasped as the heat ripped through her. She stilled for a long, sweet moment, her body arched, savoring the delicious feeling, wishing it never had to end. And then good sense returned. She had to stop him now or she was going to end up that cliché of all medical clichés: being seduced on a hospital bed by a patient. She bucked wildly beneath him, dislodging his mouth from her breast, and managing, somehow, to inadvertently jab him in the ribs with her elbow.

He grunted and loosened his hold immediately, pushing her an arm's length away to stare at her. Their gazes locked across the width of the pillow for a heated heartbeat or two, about the time it took for Quinn to finally realize her frantic writhing had had more to do with outraged womanhood than womanly passion. He let her go so suddenly that she tumbled off the side of the narrow bed.

Catlike, she caught herself before she hit the floor and landed on both feet. Straightening to her full height, she yanked her tank top up over her breast and glared down at him, trying to work up some righteous indignation with which to lambaste him for twisting her innocent offer of aid and comfort into something more physical. But indignation couldn't quite overcome the sneaking suspicion that her offer hadn't been quite as altruistic as she'd like to believe. No matter what she was feeling now, she'd never before felt compelled to crawl into a patient's bed to comfort him.

Quinn returned her speechless glare with one of his own, looking like a recalcitrant bad boy who'd been caught before he'd eaten as many peaches as he wanted from his neighbor's tree. "A simple 'No' would have been enough," he said, a suggestion of a pout on his lower lip.

"I tried that and it didn't—"

"There was no need to sucker-punch me," he complained, lifting a hand to rub his abused ribs.

Hana paled beneath her tan. "Are you in pain?" she asked, immediately switching from insulted woman to concerned physician. "Where does it hurt?" She reached out, touching the bandage over his ribs. "Here?"

"A little lower."

She moved her fingers a couple of inches lower, to where the bandage gave way to the hard flesh at the side of his waist. "Here?"

"Lower."

Hana frowned. "Lower?" she asked hesitantly. Any lower and her hand would be— She snatched her hand away.

"What's the matter, Doc?" he taunted her, his

pout turned to a bad-boy smirk. "Not your specialty?"

The righteous indignation she couldn't seem to find before came to Hana's rescue now. She glanced dismissively at the hard bulge that tented the sheet over his hips. "I don't deal with minor problems of that sort," she said coolly. "If you can't handle it yourself, I'd suggest you contact your lady of last evening to take care of it for you when you get out of here."

"I thought you were my lady of last evening."

"You thought wrong."

"Did I?" His eyebrow quirked upward. "Then how come I woke up in your bed?"

"It isn't my bed, it's a hospital bed. And you had a nightmare last night," she said, trying to be as matter-of-fact and unemotional as if she were reading from his medical chart. "You were moaning and thrashing around so much, I was afraid you'd make your injuries worse. When I tried to wake you up, you grabbed me, and—" her voice softened at the memory of his vulnerability and pain "—and you asked me not to leave you alone." Embarrassed by her emotions, she glanced away. "So I—"

His smirk widened a few insulting degrees. "So you climbed into bed with me and cradled my poor aching head to your sweet little breasts," he said sarcastically, forgetting, for the moment, that he'd previously been congratulating himself on the success of his "wounded warrior" routine. Never mind what he'd wanted from other women; the last thing he wanted from the lady doctor was pity. "Is that standard medical procedure these days?"

Hana's gaze came back to his. "No," she said, hoping her anger would conceal the hurt she felt at his unwarranted attack on her generosity. "That's standard human kindness. Something you appear to know very little about." She turned on her bare heel to leave.

A strange panic rushed through Quinn as she started to stalk away from him. He lunged up from the bed, ignoring a sharp warning from his ribs as he propped himself up on one elbow, and grabbed at her hand. "Wait. Don't—" *Don't leave me alone*, he started to say. But that was ridiculous. And embarrassing. And... He shook his head slightly. It was ridiculous, that's all.

Hana turned her head to look over her shoulder at him. "Don't?" she prompted icily, wondering why she didn't just shake loose of his hold and put an end to it. She told herself it was simply because she was curious about what he had to say; it had nothing at all to do with the lost look in his green eyes, or the way his fingers felt, wrapped around her wrist.

"Look, I'm sorry. Okay?" he said. "I didn't mean to lash out at you like that. It's just... Oh, hell, I don't know." And the truth was, he didn't. His world had been slightly off kilter from the moment she'd walked into Bennie Chu's Beachside Bar and Grill and looked down her elegant nose at him. Or *more* off kilter, anyway, than it had been for the last year and a half. He let go of her hand to plow his fingers through his disheveled hair and took a deep breath to fortify himself.

"Let's just say I'm not usually such a rotten bastard— All right," he amended, catching the skeptical look in her eyes, "maybe I am. But I'm sorry, all right?" He hunched his wide shoulders and plucked at the sheet, pulling it a little higher on his body. "It's just that I have a real hard time with pity." The expression in his eyes was hard and wary as he looked up at her, almost daring her to disagree with him. "It's a waste of emotion, and an insult. I don't need it, I don't want it and—"

"And I didn't offer it."

"What?"

"That was sympathy, not pity," she said gently. "You should learn the difference."

Quinn snorted. "There isn't any."

"Not to most men, there isn't," she agreed with a sigh. "But to women there's a world of difference between the two."

"Yeah, right."

"You can call it compassion if it will make you feel better."

"Semantics," he scoffed.

"All right, don't call it anything at all, then," she said, giving up arguing with him. Like most men, he was obviously never going to understand the finer distinctions between emotions; as a species, males didn't have the necessary vocabulary. "Just trust me when I say you're too darn big and ornery—" *not to mention good-looking* "—to be pitied. Okay?"

"Okay." He looked up at her from under his sun-bleached blond lashes, giving her one of those cajoling half smiles men have always used to wheedle women into going along with them. "Friends now?"

Hana fought not to be influenced by that smile for about two seconds, and then sighed and gave in. After all, he'd only done what any other testosterone-ridden male would do upon awaking to find a woman in bed with him, and he had stopped when he finally realized she wasn't interested in participating.

"Friends," she said, and watched his smile bloom into a full-fledged, renegade grin. *Better nip that in the bud*, she thought. "But only if you promise to behave."

"Behave?"

"Yes, behave," she said sternly. "I know it's probably a foreign concept to you." She shook her head, refusing to smile at his innocent "Who, me?" look, and laid down the rules of their newly formed friendship. "In this case, 'behaving' means following the doctor's orders. That's me," she said, tapping her chest. "It means not doing anything to complicate the patient's recovery. That's—" she placed the tip of her index finger in the middle of his chest and tried to push him back against the pillow "—you."

He resisted, covering her hand with his so that it was trapped against him, and gave her his most charming smile. The one without a smidgen of a smirk in it. "They say a kiss is the best medicine for a quick recovery."

Hana forced herself to smile, hoping her expression would hide the emotional turmoil his touch sparked in her. "Well, they're wrong, then, aren't they?" She slipped her hand out from under his as smoothly as he'd covered it. "Because you've already had a kiss and your face is still a mess." She touched the bandage over his eye. "And your ribs are still broken."

"Bruised."

"We can't know that for sure without an X-ray machine and—"

"I know for sure," he said. "They're only bruised."

"Since the only X-ray equipment in our little cluster of islands is in the hospital on Nirvana—how do you know they're only bruised?"

"I've had broken ribs before." The three lower ones on his right side, to be exact, plus a cracked pelvic bone and a right leg so badly crushed the doctors had debated taking it off just below the hip joint. "Trust me, they're just bruised."

Something in his expression prompted her to believe his diagnosis was correct. "Even so," she said, "you need a couple of days' bed rest for your body to recuperate from the trauma."

The look in his eyes turned teasing again. "What trauma is that?" he asked with a sexy little smile that left no doubt as to what trauma *he* was referring to—and it wasn't the one that had left him looking like the loser of a prizefight.

Hana responded to that smile the only way she could; she ignored it and the way it made her feel. "I'd venture to guess you're probably ready for a couple of painkillers right now," she said, pulling her doctor persona more firmly around her. "Will aspirin be enough or would you like something stronger?"

"Aspirin will be fine."

"And a cup of coffee?"

"Black."

"Would you like some toast and eggs to go with that?"

"Scrambled, please."

"The bathroom's right through that door if you need it," she said, half turning away as she spoke.

Quinn pushed himself up to a sitting position. "I was beginning to wonder," he said. Actually, he'd been planning to find it on his own as soon as she disappeared if she hadn't pointed it out first.

Hana nodded, started to leave again, then paused, knowing her medical duties weren't quite finished. *He's just like any other patient*, she told herself. *Quit acting like a teenage candy striper on her first day on the floor.* And, no matter what he said to the contrary, the man *was* hurting; she'd distinctly heard a grunt of pain when he'd pushed himself upright. "Do you feel able to make it to the bathroom on your own or would you like some help?"

Quinn thought about it for about a half a second. If he said he needed help, she'd probably bring him a damned bedpan instead of wrapping an arm around him to actually help him get to the bathroom. And he'd had enough bedpans to last him a lifetime. "I've been going to the bathroom by myself for years, now," he said. "I'll manage."

Hana stood, hovering, as he maneuvered his feet over the edge of the bed. The sheet moved with him, tangled around his legs. Hana bent to untangle it.

"I said I can manage." The words were ground out between clenched teeth.

Hana straightened without touching the sheet.

"Fine, then," she said, unconsciously backing away from the look in his eyes. "Your breakfast should be ready by the time you're back in bed."

She turned and left, walking quickly, as if she'd already totally dismissed him from her mind. At the door that separated her living quarters from the clinic she paused and, telling herself it was only a doctor's concern for her patient that prompted the action, turned to make sure he was handling the trip to the bathroom all right.

He was doing just fine. Moving a bit slowly, to be sure, but his tall, wedge-shaped body was as straight as a ship's mast, his broad shoulders were square, his head was up. He was also, except for the bandage wrapped tightly around his upper torso, as naked as the day he was born.

With an interest that wasn't the least bit professional, Hana's gaze darted down to the tightly bunched muscles of his firm male backside. It was as dark as the rest of him, tanned to the same golden brown as the flesh above and below it. *So he likes to run around naked out there on that boat of his*, she thought, smiling as her gaze wandered lower to assess the long, strong legs that carried him across the room. Her smile turned to a gasp.

Almost the entire length of his right leg was crisscrossed with scar tissue, raised and ghastly white against the sun-bronzed skin that surrounded it.

4

HER GASP HIT HIM SQUARE in the ego, hard as a physical blow, nearly causing him to trip as he stepped over the threshold into the bathroom. He grasped the door with his good hand, stopping just short of slamming it behind him, and all but stumbled over to the vanity. *Sympathy, hell,* he thought savagely, the heels of his hands pressing down hard on the edges of the porcelain sink. The knuckles of his right hand were white with the fierceness of his grip; the wound in his left hand throbbed under the pressure.

No matter what she called it, he knew the sound of *pity* when he heard it. And he didn't like it one bit. Never had. Never would. Especially not from a woman who stirred him as much as Doctor... Doctor... Dumbfounded, he raised his head and stared at himself in the mirror, realizing he didn't know her name.

He'd slept with the lady doctor in his arms, kissed her, caressed her, lusted after her with an intensity bordering uncomfortably on need, and he didn't even know her name.

"That's a bit much, Quinn," he said to the battered image staring back at him. "Even for you."

He straightened, lifting his right hand to drag it over his stubbled face, rubbing it gingerly over the

closed lids of his bloodshot eyes. Things were definitely on a downhill slide if he couldn't even remember to get the lady's name first. He must have
been drunker than he'd thought.

*"Eventually, if you keep on this way, you'll begin to
experience blackouts."* The words of the last psychiatrist the department had ordered him to see, before he'd finally said to hell with it, echoed
through his mind, taunting him with their accu-
racy. *"Drinking more and feeling it less,"* the shrink
had said. *"Textbook progression of alcoholism,"* he'd
said. And there'd been pity in his eyes when he
said it. And censure. And blame.

Oh, they all denied it, of course—every last one
of them, all the way down the line: the doctors, the
top brass, his fellow fire-fighters, the other rescue
workers, the victim's family. *"No one blames you,
Mike,"* they'd said. *"You did everything you could,"*
they'd said. *"You're a hero."*

But he knew he wasn't. And the knowledge was
eating him up inside, like an insidious, virulent
form of cancer. That's why he drank. And fought.
And whored. Drinking blurred the edges of a too-
painful reality. Fighting made him feel powerful
and fearless. And women made him forget that his
hero days were all behind him. Being with a
woman, hearing her words of flattery and praise
for his strength and prowess, seeing the admira-
tion and open desire in her eyes, feeling her body
quiver and convulse with the completion of a need
he had created, and then fulfilled, made him feel
like the man he no longer was.

And never would be again.

And that's why he hated pity so damned much.

Especially a woman's pity. Especially, he further qualified, his green eyes narrowing in to slits as he stared into the mirror, a woman doctor's pity. It made him feel as if she knew he deserved it—and why.

And he couldn't stand to have anyone knowing why. He could barely stand the knowledge of it himself. So he drank, and fought and—

"Mr. Quinn?" There was a light tap on the bathroom door. "Is everything all right?" Her voice was soft and concerned, and he knew she was thinking of the horrible scars on his leg—and *pitying* him. "Do you need any help?"

"No!" he barked. "No, I'm fine," he added, afraid she'd barge in if he didn't answer more temperately. Doctors had no respect for a man's bad mood, or his privacy, either. Mind *or* body. "Just washing up." He turned on the taps to lend credence to his statement. "I'll be out as soon as I make myself decent."

Well, thank goodness for that! Hana thought. "There are some hospital gowns in the tall metal cabinet in there," she said helpfully. "On the bottom shelf." There was a beat of silence as she waited for him to look. "Do you see them?"

"Yeah," he answered, banging open the cabinet so she'd know he was doing as he was told. Not that he had any intention of actually wearing a hospital gown. They weren't what he considered decent wearing apparel for a grown man; there was no way to retain your dignity in one, with those ridiculous ties fluttering over your bare buns and a sheepish grin on your face to hide the embarrassment. He'd walk out of the bathroom naked before he'd wear another hospital gown. Nudity, at least, had a basic, straightforward honesty about it. And—his lips turned up in a sly grin as the thought occurred to him—more than one woman had forgotten all about his scarred leg when confronted with him in all his natural glory.

"There are some new toothbrushes and things in the basket on the top shelf," Hana said through the door. "Mr. Quinn?"

"I see them," he hollered, his grin widening as he stared at himself in the mirror over the sink.

His right cross wasn't the only reason he was called the Mighty Quinn—a nickname he'd acquired *long* before he dropped anchor in Paradise—and, unless he found a towel that was bigger than the one hanging by the sink, the lucky lady doctor was going to get an eyeful of the other reason.

Good humor restored, he began to unwind the gauze from around his left hand to see what damage he'd done to himself this time.

HANA HOVERED BY THE bathroom door for a moment or two more, debating if she ought to override his protests and just go on in and help him whether he wanted her to or not, when she finally heard the sounds of splashing. She held her breath, listening, but there were no frantic calls for assistance. *Good*, she thought, relieved that she wasn't going to have to confront his nakedness, *he can handle it by himself.* "Try not to get your bandages wet," she admonished as she moved away from the door to get his breakfast.

She didn't have to go far.

Her clinic was actually a part of the small frame house she called home. Her examining room and the small hospital "ward" had, at one time, been a wide, covered porch extending across the front and along one side of the house all the way to the brick-paved, palm-tree-shaded lanai at the back. Her parents had closed the porch in to make her father's clinic when she was just a child. But that was long before her mother died and alcohol had finally claimed all of Edward Jamieson's heart and soul and ambition, leaving Hana, at the tender age of sixteen, the one to hold their lives—and the remnants of the island's only medical practice—together as best she could.

The house was old but sturdy, and when she'd returned after completing her residency to reopen her father's practice, Hana had given it a new coat of paint that went a long way toward making it look as it had when her mother was alive. It sat in splendid isolation—one small, lone house in a clearing at the end of a long, narrow, gravel drive, its privacy protected on three sides by the lush tropical growth that was typical of Paradise. On the fourth side, the undulating waves of the Pacific Ocean frothed upon the shore. The freshly painted white clapboard sides of the house matched the sugar-sand beach outside the back door; the blue trim mirrored the color of the sea.

Inside, the rooms were few and small. The two bedrooms—one of which Hana was using as an office—shared a common wall with the clinic. She had furnished the living room with rattan, Oriental prints, and bright, flowered cushions and curtains made by a local woman in exchange for medical services.

Hana walked into her sunny, hopelessly outdated kitchen that was still more than adequate for the preparation of her solitary meals. Or those of the occasional patient.

She opened the small, scrupulously clean, twenty-year-old refrigerator and absently extracted a carton of eggs and a half-full container of milk, her mind on her patient—and on her unwanted, unwelcome, completely incomprehensible reaction to him.

He was a drunk. Or, rather, she corrected herself, he'd been drunk last night. She didn't really know, for sure, if he was actually a full-fledged alcoholic. Perhaps last night was just an isolated incident. As a doctor, she shouldn't make assumptions about the man's life-style without all the facts, but as a woman whose father had suffered from the debilitating disease of alcoholism, she also operated on a much more intuitive level. The Mighty Mike Quinn might not actually be an alcoholic, but he was certainly close enough to one as should make no difference to a woman who knew, firsthand, what havoc and heartache the disease wrought in people's lives.

Hana frowned as she cracked the last of four eggs into a small earthenware bowl. If that was the case, why were her lips and breasts still tingling from the touch of a man who was, in all probability, an out-and-out drunk?

And not only a drunk, she told herself, adding a dollop of milk and beating the hapless eggs into a froth. He was a brawler, too. And a drifter. And probably a womanizer, as well, judging by the high-priced company he'd been keeping last night. A bad risk all around. And yet...

She couldn't help but wonder if his drinking and his brawling and maybe even his apparent rootlessness hadn't something to do with the raised welts and ridges on his leg and the nightmares that had turned him into a terrified child in her arms. Whatever had happened to him had left scars—not only on his leg but on his psyche. Deep scars. Possibly even debilitating scars.

Scars that could drive a man to drink? she wondered, and then shook her head as if to clear it of such nonsense.

Alcoholics didn't need to be driven to drink. If she knew anything about the disease, she knew that much. It wasn't anything anyone else did or didn't do that caused an alcoholic to drink, and it wasn't anything anyone did or didn't do that caused an alcoholic to stop drinking; it all came from inside.

It was a hard lesson, learned the hard way, but experience and therapy had finally taught her that the redeeming love of a good woman—wife, daughter or lover—was little more than a cruel myth. It was a trap she wasn't about to fall into again for anyone, let alone a drifter who'd likely—*Thank God!*—be gone on the next tide, anyway.

She struck a match and touched it to the burner under the cast-iron skillet on the stove, then shook it out with a flick of her wrist as the burner flamed. She turned to the sink and held the match under running water to make sure it was out before dropping it in the trash, idly wondering if she'd be able to douse the flame of arousal Quinn had lit inside her as easily—and thanking her lucky stars that he wasn't going to be around long enough for it to matter if she couldn't.

HANA REENTERED THE CLINIC fifteen minutes later with a laden breakfast tray, sure she'd given her patient enough time to get himself back into bed and decently covered, to find the three-bed hospital ward still empty. She put the tray down on the nearest bed and hurried toward the closed bathroom door, afraid he'd blacked out, all alone in there and sustained further injuries. *I knew I should have helped him!* She twisted the doorknob, calling his name as she pushed the door open.

"Mr. Quinn, are you all right? Have you—Oh!"

He was standing in front of the sink, still as naked as blatant sin except for the bandages that wrapped his lean midsection. Her gaze skittered downward before she could stop it. Her eyes widened. And then widened even more as his body began to react to her reaction to him. Smothering a gasp, she wrenched her gaze from his truly impressive male attributes to shoot a horrified look at his face.

He was grinning at her, the same kind of wiseass, macho-stud grin as he'd given her in the bar. It was a challenging grin, very male, making her very aware of her femaleness, daring her to…something.

"Excuse me," she said tightly, her cheeks flaming as she backed out of the bathroom.

She'd almost made it when something else caught her eye.

Her embarrassment receded in the face of more important considerations. "What in heaven's name do you think you're doing?" she said, coming back in to take the manicure scissors from his hand. "You can't take those bandages off yet."

Quinn's grin faded under the return of her professional demeanor. "They're cutting off the circulation to my lower half," he said mulishly, disappointed that her doctoring instincts were apparently stronger than her female ones.

"Humph," she snorted and glanced down again, this time as if the condition of his body concerned her only insofar as it indicated any possible medical problem. Which was true. Almost. "You don't look as if you're suffering from any lack of blood flow," she said tartly, looking back up before those other conditions could make her blush again. "Quite the opposite, I'd say."

She dropped the scissors in the sink and reached up, too concerned with surveying the damage he'd done to his bandages to notice that her words had had a somewhat deflating effect on his anatomy. Frowning, she touched the uneven edges of the three-inch cut he'd managed to hack through the thick surgical tape with the tiny manicure scissors. "I'm going to have to retape the top half of this."

She sounded as vexed as a mother whose child had deliberately put himself in harm's way after being told not to. "Here—" She put her hands on his biceps and backed him up until his legs hit the edge of the toilet. He sat down with a grunt, too startled to resist her push. "You just sit right here while I go get the tape." She slammed open the metal cabinet and yanked out a large towel. "Don't move a muscle," she ordered, dropping it on his lap, and was gone.

He sat there for half a second, staring after her retreating form, then got up, wrapped the towel securely around his hips, and followed her into the ward and past the bamboo screen that cordoned off her examining room. He was right behind her when she turned from her old-fashioned glass-fronted supply cabinet with the surgical tape and scissors in her hands. He caught her by the upper arms before her nose made contact with his breastbone.

"Don't you *ever* do what you're told?" she demanded, trying very hard not to glance down to check whether he was still naked.

"Rarely," he said. "And then only when I'm in bed with a woman—" he grinned at the annoyance on her face "—and she asks *real* nice."

"Well, I'm not prepared to get into bed with you to ensure your compliance." *However tempting the prospect.* She squirmed out of his hold, managing a quick peek downward as she did so. "So just get your tanned fanny—" *thank goodness it's decently covered* "—up on that examining table and try to cooperate, anyway."

"That didn't sound very nice," he complained, but he perched on the edge of the narrow, padded table and folded his arms over his chest.

"And that—" she nodded at his crossed arms "—doesn't look as if you're prepared to cooperate."

"If you still plan to wrap me up like King Tut, I don't."

"Meaning?"

"Meaning I'm prepared to sit still if you want to finish cutting this truss off me. Otherwise, no deal."

"Look, Mr. Quinn, I know you think your ribs are only bruised. And maybe they are. But you could be wrong. They could be broken and—"

"But they're not. And the name's just plain Quinn." His eyes gleamed. "Or Mike, if you want to get friendly."

"Okay, maybe they're only bruised," she said, ignoring the gleam—and the invitation to get friendly. "But doesn't it make sense to keep them taped until you know for sure? An ounce of prevention is worth a pound of cure and—"

"And I'm still not letting you tape me up."

Hana glared at him for an instant, using her most serious I'm-the-doctor-and-I-know-what's-best-for-you expression to intimidate him into co-operating. It didn't work. She sighed. "If I take the tape off, will you at least let me wrap an elastic bandage around you for a few days?"

He tilted his head, considering her proposal. "Well," he drawled, "since you ask so nice."

THE TAPE MADE a satisfying ripping sound as she peeled it off. Satisfying to Hana, at least, who knew that, despite all the flinching and protests of torture, it wasn't causing her patient any real pain because she'd shaved him from the nipples down before she'd taped him up. What little physical discomfort it did cause him as it pulled away from his skin was no more than a fair exchange for the mental discomfort he'd already caused her, anyway. She couldn't remember when she'd had a more contentious patient.

"It hurts less if I do it this way instead of pulling it off inch by inch," she said with what Quinn felt was a noticeable lack of concern for his suffering. "But I could do it slowly—" she dragged the word out "—if you want me to."

He glared at her. "You're enjoying this, aren't you?"

She smiled and yanked. "Yes," she said and grinned evilly when he yelped. "It serves you right for being so stubborn."

He set his lips, determined not to utter another sound that would contribute to her enjoyment, then spoiled the effect by starting when her cool fingers touched the bare skin over his ribs. She put her other palm against his chest to steady him.

He wondered if she could feel his heart thudding. Wondered, in fact, *why* it was thudding. He was supposed to be doing the seducing here, not getting seduced.

"Hurt?" she asked, probing delicately.

"Not any more than a herd of elephants would."

Hana slanted him a severe look. "Seriously?"

"No," he admitted grudgingly. "It doesn't hurt. Much," he added under his breath.

She ignored that, shifting her fingers down his rib cage at intervals of an inch or so at a time, pressing gently at each juncture and waiting for a response. When none was forthcoming, she circled his right biceps with both hands and lifted it at right angles to his body. "How about that? Hurt?" At his negative response, she slid one hand up to his shoulder, leaving the other where it was. "Can you roll your shoulder for me?"

He did. Slowly.

"Any pain?"

"Nothing I can't handle," he said in a curiously strangled voice.

Hana frowned. "I can't assess your injuries properly if you don't answer me honestly."

"That *was* an honest answer."

"Then why do you sound like you're in some kind of excruciating pain you're not telling me about?"

His answer was a disgruntled snort. *You'd think a doctor could figure it out for herself,* he thought. She was standing there running her soft little hands all over him, close enough for him to smell the flower-scented lotion she used on her skin, close enough so that the end of her long black braid brushed back and forth over his lap with every move she made, and she still had to ask. *Some doctor!*

"Well?" Hana demanded, all but tapping her foot with impatience.

Well, hell, Quinn thought. He was trying to be a gentleman but she was definitely asking for it. He quirked an eyebrow and glanced downward.

Hana's gaze followed his. "Oh." There was a noticeable bulge under the towel in his lap. "Well, that's just, um—" she swallowed "—a perfectly normal response to unavoidable physical stimulus."

Normal, except that she'd never had a male patient get an erection while she was examining him before. Not to mention that this was the third time it had happened this morning. She wondered whether he'd done it on purpose—and then immediately decided it didn't matter. Deliberate or not, the best way to handle the situation was to ignore it. *But, Lord, the man must have the constitution of a bull elephant,* she thought. *And the libido of a tomcat in permanent rut.*

She moved around the examining table to probe his injury from the back. "Hurt?" she asked, as if nothing untoward had happened.

He shrugged. "A little."

"And that?"

"No."

"Okay," she conceded. "I'll agree your ribs are probably only bruised. If you'll promise to take it easy for a while, I won't even wrap you up in an Ace bandage." She came around the examining table again as she spoke, but kept her back to him, busying herself by returning the scissors and surgical tape to her supply cabinet. "And I mean take it easy," she said sternly. "That means no brawling with Big Louie. Or anyone else, for that matter. And no other strenuous activities, like sailing." *Or sex,* she thought, somehow knowing he'd go about that particular activity as forcefully as he went about everything else. "In fact, considering all your other injuries, it would be best if you spent the next two or three days here," she said, knowing even as she said it that she was just asking for trouble but was somehow helpless to stop herself. "That way, I can keep an eye on your progress." *And your beautiful body.* "And make sure you don't overexert yourself." She sent him a quick, skittering glance over her shoulder, wondering if she sounded as lame to him as she did to herself. "Okay?"

"Okay." It was more than okay, actually; if she was keeping an eye on him, it meant that he could keep an eye on her, too. Not a difficult assignment, at all, and essential for what he had in mind, anyway. But, first, he had a point to settle.

He reached out and grasped her arm before she could move any farther away. She might say she believed his body's reaction to her was a "perfectly normal physical response," but he didn't think she believed it. "I didn't do it on purpose, Doc—" He frowned. "What the hell is your name, anyway?"

"Jamieson," she said, staring at the strong fingers wrapped around her wrist. It was infinitely safer than looking into his eyes. "Hana Jamieson."

"Well, I didn't get hard on purpose, Hana Jamieson. The first time was, well, you know what the first time was. Waking up with a woman in my arms usually has that effect on me. And, I'll admit, I was pleased you liked what you saw when you walked into the bathroom." *To put it mildly.* "As I'm sure you could tell. But I didn't plan for you to get an eyeful." *Not just then, anyway.* He'd had a much more romantic setting in mind for that. Still did. "And I didn't plan to get aroused a minute ago, either. I wasn't even *thinking* about sex." Which was almost true; he hadn't been consciously thinking about it. With her, though, he realized, it was always there, just waiting to surface. "But when you touched me…well, you're a hell of a sexy woman. So…" He shrugged, the lift of his broad shoulders sending ripples of movement down his chest. "As you said, a perfectly normal physical response." There was a long beat of silence. "Forgive me?"

"Mmm," she mumbled, still staring down at his hand on her arm. She was close enough to smell the scent of peppermint toothpaste on his breath, close enough to measure his pulse in the vein beating at the base of his strong brown throat, close enough to see that his nipples were standing at rigid attention...just like hers.

"I never meant to embarrass you." *Arouse you— yes, when the time was right. But not embarrass you.* He reached out with his other hand and lifted her chin on his curled forefinger. "Do you believe me?"

"You shouldn't have taken the bandage off," she reprimanded softly, trying to remain professional. She reached up and touched the back of his wrist, meaning to remove his hand from her chin so she could look at his palm. "The stitches aren't—"

"Never mind about my hand." He nudged her chin up a notch. "Look at me, Hana."

Slowly, willing herself not to blush, she looked up. Her gaze caressed his chin first, and then that beautiful fallen angel's mouth of his, and the sharp planes of his cheeks. His skin looked fresh and smooth, glowing with health beneath his tan, and she realized he'd shaved while he was in the bathroom. She wondered if it would feel as good against the skin of her breasts as his stubble had.

"Do you believe I never meant to embarrass you?"

She lifted her gaze a tiny fraction more and

looked into his eyes. The professionally trained part of her mind noted how well the leeches had worked—there was very little bruising beneath his eye and no swelling at all—and wondered whether it was excess alcohol or pain and troubled dreams that made the whites of his eyes so bloodshot.

The female part of her brain was struck by the unique beauty of his clear green irises and the sun-bleached paleness of his short, spiky lashes. There were fine lines radiating from the corners of his eyes, laugh lines and squint lines, lines of pain and character, etched into the deep tan of his face, saving him from being too theatrically good-looking and making him beautiful instead.

"Do you believe me?" he repeated. It was important, suddenly, that she believed him. Which was funny because he hadn't really cared about anyone's believing him in a long time, not even in a matter as simple and relatively unimportant as this. Except that this seemed very important. "Hana?"

"Yes," she replied. The sincerity in his eyes left no room for doubt. "Yes, I do."

"And you don't hold my, uh, physical reactions against me?"

"No."

"That's good. That's real good."

He should have let her go then, but he didn't. She should have pulled away, but she couldn't. Very slowly, giving her every chance to avoid it if she wanted to, he brought her head closer with the finger under her chin. She let him, flowing toward him like a sea anemone in an ocean current. Her rosy lips were half parted, her eyelids drooping closed in delicious anticipation of the taste of him.

"Hana," he murmured softly, just as his lips touched hers.

The short, sharp blast of a car horn sliced through the quiet of the office, causing them to jerk apart like children caught playing doctor. A car door slammed just outside the clinic. Footsteps crunched across the gravel drive and up the wooden steps.

Hana blushed and whirled back toward the supply cabinet. Quinn cursed and reached down to make sure the towel was decently closed over his lap.

There was a sharp rap on the clinic door as it opened. "Hana? You here?"

It was Bennie.

"I'm—" She cleared her throat and started over. "I'm in the examining room," she called out, "with a pa—"

"I wanted to make sure you weren't having any trouble with that Quinn—" he rounded the dividing screen "—fella." His eyes darted back and forth between the half-naked man on the examining table and the young woman he loved like a sister. They were both flushed. Bennie's eyes narrowed. "He giving you any trouble, Hana?"

"No, of course not. We were just, um—" she flicked a guilty glance at Quinn "—finishing up."

Quinn shook his head at her, negating her statement without saying a word. *"Just starting" was more like it,* he thought.

Flustered by his knowing look, Hana turned her attention back to the supply cabinet, though, for the life of her, she couldn't have said what she was looking for—or at. "We don't seem to have any clean hospital gowns in here," she said. "I'll have to get one from the bathroom."

"I'd rather have my clothes."

"I had to cut your shirt off," she said, still without looking at him. Or Bennie. "And your jeans need to be washed. They have blood on them."

"They've had worse on them." He sighed and eased himself down off the examining table. "Hana." Ignoring Bennie, he put his hand on her shoulder and turned her around. "I'm not going to press it now," he said softly, staring down into her eyes. "It isn't the time or the place. But I *am* going to press it. Soon."

"Press it?"

"You know exactly what I mean. I want you," he said baldly, the words seeming all the more intense and meaningful for being spoken in a whisper. "Very much."

Speechless, she shook her head in a tiny fraction of a movement that was hardly a movement at all.

"Yes," he said. "And what I want, I usually get." And then, because he couldn't resist it, he planted a quick, hard kiss on the incredulous "O" of her mouth. "And that's a promise, Doc."

As he walked away from her, past Bennie and around the screen into the ward, he felt her eyes on his bare back. He hitched the towel up around his hips, making absolutely no effort to tone down the swagger in his step. This time, he knew, she wasn't thinking of his scarred leg or his nightmares or anything else but what it was going to be like when he kept the sensual promise he'd just made her. Because, no matter how hard she tried to pretend otherwise, Dr. Hana Jamieson wanted him, too. Almost as much as he wanted her.

He was grinning to himself, reaching for the jeans draped over the foot of his bed and thinking of just how it was going to be, when Bennie spoke from behind him.

"I don't know what all that whispering was about in there," he said. "Hana wouldn't say. And I don't figure you will, either. But I can guess. And I don't like it."

Quinn buttoned the last button on his jeans and turned around. "You got some claim on her I should know about?"

"She's my cousin," he said, neglecting to mention just how distant the relationship really was.

"And?"

"And if you hurt her, I'll make sure you regret it."

Quinn didn't make the mistake of doubting him. The other man might be smaller but he wasn't soft, and there was a look in his eyes that said he'd seen—and done—more than his share of living on life's rougher edges. Quinn nodded. "I'm not planning on hurting her." He probably would, sooner or later, but he wasn't planning on it.

"Plan or not, you remember what I said." Bennie dropped a piece of paper on the narrow bed.

Quinn raised an eyebrow.

"Your half of the damages to my bar."

5

HANA WAITED, AS NERVOUS as a first-year intern, for Quinn to "press it." She didn't know what she'd do when he did. *Succumb?* she wondered, admitting to herself that, based on the way she'd already reacted to him despite the stern talking-to she'd already given herself—and continued giving herself whenever she felt her heartbeat falter— it was a possibility that had to be considered. An unbelievable possibility, given her background and his two-fisted, footloose, hard-drinking way of life. An unthinkable possibility, except that she was thinking about it far too seriously for her peace of mind. A frightening, exciting, thankfully remote but nevertheless quite distinct possibility.

She tried to make it even more remote by resolving to treat him just like any other patient for the few days he would be—through her own stupidity, no less!—a resident in her clinic. Unfortunately, Quinn refused to act like any other patient Hana had ever had.

The deferential respect she was used to getting from her patients—that certain diffident attitude that clearly set the boundaries of the patient-doctor relationship even when the patient in question had known her since her elementary-school days—was missing in Quinn. Not that he was disrespectful of either her or her professional skills. It was nothing so blatant as that. He just didn't view them with the proper...*reverence* was the only word she could think of. And he didn't have a diffident bone in his whole battered, gorgeous body.

He refused to wear the hospital gown she offered him Sunday morning. "My jeans'll do me just fine," he insisted, having managed to rinse out the bloodstains in the bathroom sink.

He also refused the old shirt of her father's she'd dug out of an old trunk full of her parents' things. "Too small," he said, which was true. "And it irritates my skin," he added, scratching at the golden stubble on his tanned chest.

Which meant she was faced with his broad, bare torso just about every time she turned around because he wouldn't stay in bed, either, except when he was actually sleeping. And he didn't do *that* nearly often enough for her peace of mind.

"It's not as if I'm really sick," he said reasonably when she remonstrated him. "I'm just supposed to be 'taking it easy,'" he reminded her, unabashedly using her own words of the day before against her. "Besides, I'd drive myself crazy if I stayed in bed all day. You, too," he added with a grin.

Hana looked at him out of the corner of her eye, trying to judge whether he meant the remark as some sort of double entendre, but his green gaze was as guileless as a child's—despite the killer grin—and she was forced to conclude that the implication was all in her suddenly sex-obsessed mind.

That being the case, she set herself the task of

avoiding temptation for the rest of the day, finding a myriad time-consuming and essentially unnecessary things to do in her stuffy little office rather than spend her Sunday on her own lanai or lazing on the beach that ran from the edge of the faded red bricks to the blue waters of the Pacific Ocean. In her absence, the Mighty Quinn appropriated her hammock, his big, bruised body stretched out in the leafy shade of an overhanging palm while she sweltered inside. Hana's only consolation was the knowledge that her files had never been in such good order.

ON MONDAY THERE WAS an accident out at the site of the new high-rise hotel complex on the southernmost shore of Paradise. Hana couldn't help but view it as a mixed blessing. On the one hand, it gave her a legitimate reason to avoid her distressingly ambulatory patient without having to admit that that's what she was doing. On the other hand, she would have preferred not to have anything to do with the new hotel at all. She'd lobbied against it when the off-island developers had first proposed it, on the grounds that Paradise already had as much tourist traffic as it could handle with the avid sports fishermen and scuba divers that sought out their shores every year; they didn't need the problems thousands more visitors would bring—even if they brought thousands of tourist dollars with them. Predictably, most of the good citizens of Paradise hadn't agreed with her, and so the hotel was going up. She didn't like it, but... She was a doctor and people were hurt. She told Quinn and her receptionist-cum-secretary-cum-assistant, Kim, that she'd most likely be gone for the rest of the afternoon, and went where she was needed.

It was long after the spectacular tropical sunset when Quinn finally heard the wheels of her van crunch over the gravel drive, signaling her return. He heard her car door bang—loudly—followed by the sound of her sneakered feet stomping up the broad front steps and across the wooden floor of the clinic. A light went on when she reached her examining room, throwing patterns of brightness over the bricks of the lanai, pushing the evening shadows deeper into the darkness beneath the palm trees where Quinn lay.

Stretched out on the hammock, he stayed where he was for a moment longer, listening to Hana swear as she slammed around her examining room. The clapboard walls of the house were thin, as was often the case in tropical climates, and both the window and the door were open to let in the ocean breezes, allowing him to hear every furious word with amazing clarity.

He grinned at the good doctor's ladylike choice of swearwords, deploring the apparent fact that no one had ever seen fit to teach her the proper idioms for expressing her anger more forcefully. He set his beer down on the bricks by the hammock and got to his feet, fully intending to fill that gap in her education and, hopefully, turn her anger to his advantage—and hers, if she was honest enough to admit it.

Anger, after all, was just another kind of passion; oftentimes as exhilarating in its own way as the kind that led more directly to sex. He wondered if she'd be as passionate about a man—about *him*—as she so obviously was about the conditions on her island home. It was an exciting possibility, especially when he considered how ardently she'd responded the other morning when she was still half asleep.

No doubt about it, Quinn thought, listening to her rant and rave and bang things around, the lady doctor was a real firecracker under all that professional starch. He couldn't wait to feel her explode in his arms.

With that thought uppermost in his mind, he ambled over to the doorway of the examining room. Entering only just as far as the doorjamb, he tucked his hands into the front pockets of his low-riding jeans and slouched against the blue-painted frame. "What's the matter, Doc?"

Hana didn't even jump up at the sound of his voice. "Nothing's up to code at that hotel," she said, fuming. She knew she was probably being unfair about that—they had to be adhering to *some* kind of building code—but she was too furious to care about fairness just then. "Or nothing would be," she went on, enjoying the chance to vent her frustration on something besides the inanimate objects in her examining room, "if Paradise had a code. Which we don't."

Quinn crossed his arms over his bare chest and gave her a mildly incredulous look. "Paradise doesn't have a building code?"

"Oh, we do, but it isn't very—" she waved a hand, looking for a word, and, for once in the short time she'd known him, not the least bit distracted by his naked chest "—comprehensive," she decided. "And it's never actually been enforced. There's been no need. Gaston's Chandlery is—was," she added, thinking of the new hotel, "the biggest building on the island, and it's been there forever. Everything else is one-story construction. Even the Paradise Motel is just a cluster of small picturesque units around a waterfall and an oversize lanai. Nothing really fancy on the whole island, if you don't count all the gingerbread on CeeCee's Surf Shop and Bikini Boutique. It used to be a whalers' brothel," she added by way of explanation. "So who needs a formal building code? According to the island council—" her lip curled into a close approximation of a sneer "—Paradise certainly doesn't. That damned hotel is going to be the death of this island if we're not careful. In more ways than one."

Quinn made encouraging noises, enjoying the fireworks display—and fully expecting some of the fire to be turned his way when she quit raging about things she couldn't change.

"The developers aren't even from Paradise," she said, as if it were a personal affront. "They don't care about its culture or economics. Or any of its people. All they care about is making as much money as fast as possible."

"It is the American way," Quinn murmured, goading her.

Hana glared at him. "Capitalist." She made it sound like the vilest sort of perversion.

He grinned. "No need to get nasty," he said, levering himself away from the doorway. He came across the room and put his hands on the lapels of her blood-spattered lab coat, pushing it off her shoulders before she could think to protest. "You can disinfect this later," he said, tossing it across the examining table as if it were contaminated with the Black Death. "Right now—" he took her slender hand in his and drew her along behind him "—come on inside and I'll give you a beer to relax you and you can tell me what happened to make you look as if you'd been working in a slaughterhouse."

"No, thanks. I don't like it," Hana said.

"What?" Quinn glanced over his shoulder at her. "Beer?"

"Anything alcoholic."

"Okay. No beer," he said easily, leading her out onto the moonlit lanai. "We'll try a back rub, instead. That's just as relaxing as a beer." *And it gives me a reason to put my hands on you.*

Hana had just enough presence of mind to resist being guided to the hammock; no way was she going to let him give her a back rub, no matter how tempting it sounded. She plunked herself down on a squeaky cane patio chair instead. Quinn shrugged and went around behind her. He brushed her braid out of the way and put his hand on her nape. She jumped.

"Relax. I'm not going to bite you." *Not yet, anyway.* "I'm just going to massage some of that tension away. One-handed," he said, tacitly reminding her that the other hand was injured and, thus, harmless. He picked up his beer in his injured hand, enjoying the feel of the cold can against his palm, and squeezed her neck lightly with the other. "Relax," he said again, wobbling her head from side to side. "You're as tight as a drum."

Hana moaned softly and let her head fall forward.

The Mighty Quinn grinned into the night over her head. The old Quinn magic was working already and he hadn't even gotten started. "Tell me what happened over at the hotel today."

"One of the beams came loose," she said into her chest. "Or maybe it hadn't been completely fastened yet—it was still attached to a crane. I don't know. Anyway, three men were injured. Two were fairly minor—abrasions and contusions. The third man had a nasty gash on his head and was out cold. I was able to stop the bleeding. Finally. But I couldn't bring him around. We had to airlift him to the hospital on Nirvana."

"Those head wounds can bleed like a son of a bitch," Quinn said, thinking of her blood-smeared coat.

"Yes." She sighed, partly in sadness at the memory of the afternoon, partly in pure animal enjoyment of Quinn's kneading hand on her nape. He had a lovely touch; firm but not too firm, squeezing her tense muscles without pinching, generating a soothing warmth that turned her spine to jelly. It was the technique of someone who'd been massaged himself, probably quite often, and, as a result, knew what felt good and what didn't. *Physical therapy?* she wondered, recalling the scars on his right leg.

"Have you fallen asleep on me?" His voice was as warm and lazy as the hand on her neck.

"No." She drew the word out. "I was just wondering."

"About what?"

She hesitated briefly. "About your leg."

His hand stilled for half a second, then started squeezing again. "What about it?"

"How did it happen?"

"I was in an accident."

"Motorcycle?" She'd worked in enough emergency rooms during her residency in Los Angeles to recognize the results of a limb that had been pinned under the weight of a sliding motorcycle. As extensive as his injuries had appeared to be, it was a wonder he hadn't lost his leg.

Quinn was almost tempted to let her believe it. "Not a motorcycle," he said, resolving to tell her the truth—or as much of the truth as he'd told anyone since he'd left the department. "Collapsed building."

Hana turned her head to look up at him. "Collapsed building?"

He used the pressure of his hand to turn her head back so that she was looking at her lap again. "You recall that big quake in California?" he asked, continuing to massage her neck as if the subject they were discussing hadn't altered his whole life. "The one about eighteen months ago?"

She was suddenly glad he couldn't see her face. "You were in that?"

"I'm—" His brief hesitation was slight but telling. "I was a fire fighter. My unit was specially trained for heavy rescue work. When 'the big one' hit, it was our job to dig the city out of it." His voice went curiously flat. "I was inside a partially collapsed building when the first aftershocks hit."

"And you were trapped inside," she said, horrified. She closed her eyes. "Oh, my God," she breathed, very quietly.

"Yeah, well…" She could feel his shrug. "I lived through it."

But at what cost? she wanted to say. *At what terrible, terrible price?* She understood the nightmares now; the muttered, guttural cries about being held down in the dark, gasping for air and unable to breathe. She thought that maybe she understood a lot more, too. Like the brawling and the drinking, and the cocky I-can-take-on-all-comers attitude. But she didn't dare say so. She already had ample evidence that the Mighty Quinn was a man who didn't take easily to offers of sympathy.

"You were lucky," she said simply.

He'd heard that before, and he wondered now, as he had then, if he'd ever feel that way about it. Lucky wasn't a word he thought he'd ever be able to apply to that day. Catastrophic, life-altering; tremendously, cataclysmically destructive; but not lucky. Never lucky. His hand stilled on her neck.

Hana lifted her head. "Mike?"

He answered her with a soft, absent "Hmm?" lost in his memories of that fateful day, unaware that it was the first time she'd called him anything but Mr. Quinn. Even in the moonlight and shadows, she thought, the pain was clearly visible on his chiseled face.

Hana's soft heart contracted. Her generous soul ached to ease him. "Mike, I…"

His gaze sharpened, his eyes narrowing at her tone. She was about to offer pity.

Hana swallowed and went on, knowing what

that look meant; knowing, too, that she had to try, anyway. "If you'd like to talk about it, I'd like to listen. It sometimes helps to ease the pain if you can talk about it."

Quinn knew from vast experience that it didn't. Nothing helped. Nothing but fighting and drinking and sex. He smiled down at her and slid his hand from her nape to the side of her neck so that the tips of his fingers were resting along the slender column of her throat. "Are you offering to comfort me?" he asked, sliding his hand down so that his little finger brushed back and forth across her fragile upper chest, along the very edge of her tank top.

Hana sat very still. "I'm offering to be friends," she said stubbornly, trying valiantly to ignore the trail of fire his finger stroked across her skin. He might not think he needed a friend but he did. Desperately. And she could be that friend, if he'd let her get close enough.

"Men and women can't be friends, honey. Didn't you know that? But you can still comfort me." His smile widened into a grin. The same sly, cocksure, macho grin he'd given her in the bar. The one full of suggestion and innuendo and sex. "In bed."

Though she'd known what was coming, Hana stiffened. With anger. With outrage. With desire.

"Or you could comfort me out here on the lanai. That hammock—" he tilted his head toward it "—looks more than strong enough to stand up under some heavy—" his husky voice lowered suggestively "—breathing. How 'bout it, Hana?" He let his hand drop, his little and ring fingers just brushing under the edge of her tank top now, grazing the uppermost curves of her breasts, his thumb unerringly finding the pulse at the base of her throat. It fluttered against the pad of his thumb like a frightened hummingbird. "Want to find out the real reason they call me the Mighty Quinn?"

Oh, she was tempted. Lord, how she was tempted. But she wasn't about to be bullied into bed—or a hammock—by any man. Not even one who was hurting so bad he had to strike out at others. She stood, throwing his hand off as she rose. "I'm going to bed now," she said. "Alone." The look in her eyes challenged him to stop her.

He knew he could have. One touch, one kiss, and he could have. She might resist him at first, might make a coy, token protest to preserve her self-respect and give herself a reason to blame him when it was over, but then she would have turned to shimmering fire in his arms. He knew women, and he knew Hana Jamieson was his if he wanted her.

And he did. Desperately. It amazed him just how desperately. But not like this, he realized with unexpected insight. Not because she couldn't say no. Not because he'd overwhelmed her with sensations and needs and her yearning body was overriding the dictates of her mind. Suddenly he realized he had a bellyful of regrets and shame and enough of sex for sex's sake. He wanted Hana to say yes and mean it with everything in her. But he could wait—at least for one more night.

He stepped back, making her a clipped little bow as she brushed past him. The door closed behind her as she went inside.

He took a long pull on his beer and then another, draining it. He'd purchased a six-pack at the little Mom-and-Pop grocery store a couple of miles down the beach while Hana was out being a Good Samaritan. He popped the tab on another one. It was cold comfort and, somehow, it didn't taste nearly as good as it had before she'd joined him out on the lanai, but it was all he had. After the first couple of sips, he pushed the beer away in disgust, electing to take another walk down the deserted beach instead.

HANA WAS DOING HER BEST to ignore the Mighty Quinn the next afternoon.

He was out on her lanai, still "taking it easy," as she'd impulsively advised him to do when she patched him up—taking shameless advantage of her hospitality when she knew he could have taken it just as "easy" back on his sloop. He lazed in her comfortable old hammock, listening while she conducted her regular prenatal class on the sugar-sand beach that was her backyard. He was barefoot and bare-chested, his indecently tight, faded jeans riding low on his lean hips, his arms folded up behind his head so that the roped muscles of his biceps and triceps stood out in sharp relief and his belly was stretched to concave nothingness.

The bruise on his ribs had already faded from hideous purple to an ugly yellow-green. Hana had taken out his stitches that morning—both above his eye and in his hand—after a cursory examination had confirmed his claim of being an unusually fast healer. He'd pulled her straw beach hat low over his face, and one long leg was bent at the knee, dangling over the edge of the hammock. Every so often, as if to call her attention to himself and remind her that he was still there, he pushed against the warm bricks of the lanai with his toes and set the hammock swaying.

It was a big, wide, luxurious hammock, with an equally wide, faded-blue futon covering the webbed ropes. It had been hanging in that very spot, suspended between the house and a huge old palm tree, ever since she was a child. She used to lie between her parents in that hammock during the good times, years ago before her mother had died and her father had gotten really bad, staring up through the leafy palm fronds at a starry sky. These days, she lay in it by herself when she had time, much as Quinn was doing now, the rhythmic creaking of rope against wood bringing back that wonderful childhood feeling of safety and contentment. At the moment, though, all she could think about was whether the old ropes would hold up under the more vigorous activity that Quinn had suggested last night. Which caused her, more than once, to lose the thread of what she was saying to the expectant mothers in this week's session of her prenatal class.

"By the eighth month the fetus is—ah, the fetus is about five pounds and will have developed—" Was that a grin she saw from under the brim of the hat shading his face? "Developed almost everything it needs to survive in the world outside its mother's womb." Yes, it was definitely a grin. The kind of grin that said he knew exactly what she was thinking. *The wretch.*

Hana shifted her position on the sand, making it look as if the movement were necessary to show everyone in the class the chart she was holding. When she settled again, Quinn was no longer in her direct line of sight. *Out of sight, out of mind,* she thought, lying to herself; but it allowed her to go on with her lecture without tripping over her tongue. "Often the only apparent difference between an eight-month preemie and a full-term baby is one of size. And, in the majority of cases, there's no reason a baby born four or even six or eight weeks early can't thrive. With, of course, the proper care. But, as I've said before—" she looked into the faces of the women seated in a semicircle around her to make sure they all understood the importance of what she was saying "—if there are any complications, if the baby needs any special treatment or equipment, if any of you need special treatment or equipment, well—" she spread her hands "—we don't have it here on Paradise. And those of you like Kathy—" she nodded at an over-thirty-five mother whose enormous belly evidenced the fact that she was expecting twins "—or Darlene—" she let her gaze rest on another young woman who'd been brought to the class by her mother "—will need to make arrangements to go to the hospital on Nirvana. And the sooner, the better. Don't put it off until you feel the first contractions coming on. The emergency helicopter may be busy or the weather may be bad, so you should make arrangements to be over there at least two weeks, all right, a week," she amended when one of the women protested, "before your due date."

"My husband says women have been having babies on Paradise without any special equipment for at least a thousand years," Darlene said. "He says there's no need to go all the way to Nirvana just to have a baby."

She was eighteen years old, outwardly healthy and fit as she entered her seventh month of pregnancy, despite the fact that her macho, back-to-nature husband hadn't seen the need for the special prenatal vitamins Hana had prescribed. He also hadn't understood what all the fuss was about over Darlene's increasing blood pressure, nor had he agreed to the special tests Hana had recommended—tests that could only be done at the hospital on Nirvana. Hana considered his attitude over his wife's pregnancy just another manifestation of his shortsightedness; that he was also working a construction job at the new hotel complex was another.

"In most cases your husband would be right," Hana agreed smoothly, not wanting to give Darlene an excuse for refusing to come to class. It was clear she was only there only at her mother's insistence. "Most women deliver healthy babies with no problems at all. But your case is special, Darlene," she said, not going into specifics in front of the group, "and you'll need special care to have a successful pregnancy and delivery."

"And she'll get it," Darlene's mother said, with a stern look at her daughter. "No matter what that no 'count husband of hers says."

"Oh, Ma..." The young woman's voice faded to a furious whisper.

"Well," Hana said, ignoring the low-voiced argument going on between mother and daughter, "does anyone have any questions on today's subject? No? Well, then—" she tossed her braid back behind her and stood "—I'll see you next Tuesday." She stretched out both hands to help two of the more ponderously pregnant women to their feet. "Anyone who hasn't already done so, please check with Kim to confirm your next appointment." She put her arm around the shoulders of the woman who was expecting twins. "Why don't you go on into the examining room and get into a gown? I'll be along in a minute," she said, squeezing Kathy's shoulders lightly before she let her go.

Bending over, Hana picked her pasteboard charts up off the sand, shook them and tucked them under her arm. Brushing sand off her hands as she crossed the lanai, she glanced down at Quinn to see if he'd observed the thorough professionalism with which she'd handled her class despite the silent distraction of his presence.

"Why didn't you just tell her her husband is a dumb jerk?" Quinn said from under the straw hat, letting her know he'd listened to every word.

"Like all men, you mean?" Hana said sweetly.

He tipped the hat back with his thumb, acknowledging her hit with a grin. "No. Seriously."

"I *was* serious," Hana said, her lips twitching in an answering grin. And then she sobered. "I didn't tell her her husband was a dumb jerk because she's got a serious health problem and if I alienate her, she might not come back," she said.

"How serious?"

"Serious enough that there's a chance she could have a stroke, or even die, during a prolonged or difficult labor. And that's *with* all the proper emergency equipment on hand. Here on Paradise, without any emergency equipment, the chance is much worse."

"Does she know that?"

"Of course, she knows," Hana said. "I believe in being totally up-front with my patients." She sighed and shook her head. "But she's young. She thinks it won't happen to her."

"Maybe it won't," Quinn said, but he didn't really believe it.

"Maybe," Hana agreed, but she didn't believe it, either.

They stared at each other for a heartbeat's worth of time; Quinn, seemingly at ease in the hammock, the afternoon sunlight trickling down through the palm fronds to dapple his face and chest; Hana, standing on the hot bricks in the full glare of the sun, her shoulders seeming much too slender for the awesome responsibilities she carried.

"You care too much, Doc," Quinn said softly.

Hana held his gaze for a moment longer, trying to read the expression in his eyes. "So do you," she said, knowing it was true.

"IS THAT GORGEOUS HUNK in your hammock the man who got into a fight with Big Louie at Bennie's last Saturday night?" Kathy asked when Hana came into the examining room.

And that, thought Hana, was both the joy and the bane of doctoring people you'd known all your life. They might treat your profession with the proper reverence and respect, but they felt entirely free to poke into any other area of your life.

"Well," Kathy prompted when Hana didn't answer. "Is he?"

"I don't know about 'gorgeous,'" Hana said, conscious of the screened window that opened out onto the lanai, "but that's him."

"Don't know about gorgeous? Hana, are you blind? The man looks like some kind of Viking god." Kathy pushed the sleeve of her gown up out of the way as Hana unfolded a blood-pressure cuff. "What a bod," she said, holding out her arm. "Shoulders out to there. Great chest. Washboard stomach. And those arms! As thick and hard as young palm trees." She sighed deeply. "I bet they'd feel *wonderful* wound all around a woman."

Hana censored her with a look. "I'm sure your husband would just love to hear you talk about another man like that," she chided.

Kathy's dark eyes twinkled. "Dan wouldn't care. Not as long as the only man I actually let wind himself around me is him. Besides, he knows I've had sex on the brain lately and he doesn't hold anything I say against me. Being pregnant always brings out the female in me. Raging hormones," she said with a sage nod. "So—" She slanted a sly glance up at Hana. "Is the lower half as good?"

"The lower half of what?"

"The lower half of your Viking god. Is it as good as the top half?"

"I wouldn't know," Hana lied, and hoped she wasn't blushing. Hoping, too, that Quinn wasn't listening. She pumped up the blood-pressure cuff and cursed the island climate and the lack of air-conditioning that made open windows necessary for comfort.

"You mean to tell me you didn't use your God-given right as a doctor to get him naked when you had the chance?" Kathy shook her head. "You've got more willpower than I do."

"Which is probably why you're expecting twins at thirty-six. Now, be quiet a minute." Hana inserted the earpieces of her stethoscope into her ears and applied the other end to the bend of her patient's elbow. "Normal," she said after a moment. She slipped off the cuff, motioned her patient to keep quiet a bit longer, and took the mother-to-be's pulse. "And normal." She draped the stethoscope around her neck and put her hands on her patient's shoulders. "Lie back now."

MUCH LATER THAT EVENING, after her last patient had left and her receptionist had gone for the day, Hana stepped out onto the lanai. The sun was just disappearing into a pink-and-gold sea, leaving Paradise shadowed in the twilight of a tropical evening. The air was like velvet, soft and warm. The sound of the waves, breaking softly against the sand, was like a soothing, seductive lullaby. And the Mighty Mike Quinn was nowhere to be seen.

Hana made straight for the empty hammock. With a grateful sigh, she kicked off her thongs and sank down into its comforting embrace, snuggling her backside into the worn futon as she stretched her arms over her head.

"I thought doctors took some sort of oath about lying," Quinn said, his disembodied voice floating out of the shadows of the palm trees at the edge of the lanai.

Hana halted in midstretch and peering into the shadows, trying to pinpoint his position. "Lying about what?"

"About whether or not you'd used your 'God-given right as a doctor' to get me naked."

"As I recall, you got yourself naked," she said tartly. "More than once."

"And you looked. More than once. So what's the verdict, Doc?" His tone was intimate, suggestive, unbearably arousing. He stepped onto the lanai. "Is my bottom half as gorgeous as the rest of me?"

Lord, yes! Hana thought, and then bit her tongue. She sat up and swung her legs over the edge of the hammock, turning to face him so she could make a quick getaway—should it become necessary.

"Don't get up on my account," Quinn said. "I'm not going to jump you."

"I didn't think you were."

"Liar," he chided. "And you with your Hippocratic oath and all."

She could hear the teasing note in his voice and felt her own lips turning up in an answering grin. "The Hippocratic oath doesn't say anything about lying. And I didn't think you were going to 'jump me.'" She gave him a look of affronted innocence. "The thought never even crossed my mind."

"Yes, it did." He sauntered across the lanai. Light shone out through the open windows, high-lighting his blond hair and outlining the sharp angles of his face, but his features were shadowed.

His fingers were tucked into the front pockets of his jeans. His chest and feet were still bare. "You thought I was going to pounce on your luscious bones the minute I caught you alone. That's why you've been avoiding me."

"That's ridiculous."

"But you thought it." He was close enough now so that she could see his teasing, roguish smile. "And you've been thinking about it all day. I know, because I've been thinking about it, too." And thinking about it...and thinking about it...until it was about to drive him crazy.

He looked down at her, his smile fading. He took one hand out of his pocket and ran his knuckles down the softness of her cheek. "Have you ever made love in a hammock, Hana?"

Get up, she told herself. *Run.* But she didn't. "No."

"Would you like to?"

"No," she said again but she sat very still under his stroking touch.

"Liar, liar, pants on fire," he taunted softly as he sank down on the edge of the hammock next to her and took her hand in his. He lifted it to his lips, turned it over and pressed a hot, openmouthed kiss into her palm. It seared right through to the bone. "Are your pants on fire, Hana?"

Yes. Oh, God, yes! she thought, closing her eyes against the blazing heat. *And my breasts and my lips and every inch of skin right down to my feet.* She curled her toes against the warm bricks and bit back a whimper.

"I'm on fire, too, Hana. I'm a damned raging inferno. And you're what started it."

"I thought it was somebody named Angel who did that."

"If it'd been Angel, I'd have gone to Angel to put it out," he said, and she believed him. "It's you I need."

Oh, God. *Need.* If he'd said *want* or *desire...* But he'd said "need" in that whiskey-soft, yearning voice—in that voice he probably didn't even know was yearning—and she couldn't resist. Didn't even want to try to resist. If he pushed, even a tiny bit more, she'd melt like a chocolate bar left in the sun. She waited—tense, anxious, trembling—for him to push that extra bit more that would send her tumbling into mindless passion.

And then Quinn put her hand back in her lap. "But it's up to you," he said. He clasped his hands together between his knees and stared down at them. "I'm not going to seduce you into something you'll regret. You have to tell me you want me, too."

He'd put it squarely in her lap, she thought, dismayed. Instead of seducing her into mindless acquiescence, which he so easily could have done, he'd made it her decision. And if there were any regrets in the morning, she would have only herself to blame. The man was either very, very clever, or so consumed by whatever demons he carried inside that he wasn't thinking clearly.

She lifted her hand to his cheek and turned his face to hers so she could look into his eyes. Hell looked back at her. The hell of his past. Of his pain. Of something she couldn't name. Hell wrapped in yearning, wrapped in needs so vast she couldn't comprehend them all. "Mike, I..." She didn't know what to say, how to soothe him. And she wanted, very much, to soothe him, to wipe away that tortured look.

His hands were clasped so tightly together his knuckles were white. His broad shoulders were hunched as if to take her refusal. "Your decision."

And suddenly it was easy.

She slid her hand around to the back of his head, threading her fingers through his hair. "Yes," she said softly, and brought his mouth down to hers.

6

FOR ALL THE HEAT and suppressed passion simmering between them, it was a curiously gentle kiss—at first. Her lips touched his, offering a sweetness and warmth that he responded to like a living thing too long deprived of rain or sunshine. They stayed like that for a moment or two, sitting side by side on the hammock in the deepening twilight, connected by the warmth of their lips and her hand on the back of his head. And then he unclasped the hands he had been clasping together to keep from reaching for her, and surged forward, like a wave upon the shore, his hands on her shoulders, pressing her back against the faded-blue futon that covered the old hammock.

And still their lips clung, mouths open now, breath mingling, tongues seeking. He slid his hands from her shoulders to her neck and up to her head, tilting it back, cupping her face in his palms to hold her, just so, for his voracious mouth. He couldn't get enough of the taste of her. The softness. The heat. The sweetness. She was everything that was womanly and forgiving, everything he had ever needed. He feasted on her, nibbling and licking at her lips, swirling his tongue into her mouth only to withdraw it to nibble at her again, kissing her with such single-minded concentration that it seemed as if he would be content just to hold her head in his hands and do nothing but taste her the whole night long.

Hana lay acquiescent beneath him, returning his hot, consuming kisses, languorous with surprise, swamped with delight. She'd half expected him to fall on her like a ravenous beast, to tear off her clothes, perhaps, in his haste to sate his terrible need in her. She'd been ready for that. More than ready. But this was... It was everything a kiss should be; intimate and tender, carnal and hot, and so sweet she wanted to cry. It was like floating on a sea of delicious sensation, buoyed by his tender hands and avid, seeking mouth, anchored by the big, hard body poised over hers. She felt delicate and strangely cherished by this scarred and hurting man, as if she were a much-desired and long-awaited prize he'd finally won. It made her feel more wanted, more needed at an elemental female level, than she'd ever felt in her life. She sighed into the mouth so gently plundering hers, wanting it to go on forever.

His hands left her face, trailing down her body to cup her breasts through the light cotton fabric of her blouse. Balancing on both elbows, he lifted his lips from hers to press tiny, hot kisses all over her face. "Beautiful Hana," he crooned, his thumbs strumming across her nipples as his lips brushed across her cheek. "Sweet, sweet Hana."

She moaned, arching into his touch as her arms tightened around his neck, wanting that sweet torment to go on forever, too.

"Hot Hana," he said, and claimed her mouth again.

It was a different kiss now. More forceful. More fervent. Deeper. His plundering tongue moved faster, blatantly imitating the act of intercourse, and Hana's languor vanished into the warm night air. All the muscles in her thighs softened in anticipation and heated need. She bent her knees, moving them wider apart as she braced her bare feet on the edge of the hammock, brazenly inviting a more intimate contact.

Quinn accepted her silent invitation with alacrity, thrust his jeans-clad hips forward and ground his erection against her. Hana whimpered and lifted her hips even higher, blindly seeking to guide him to where she needed the pressure most, moaning when he found exactly the right spot.

It sufficed for only a minute or two—that hot, sweet incredible pressure, that slow grinding of male against female, that promise of deeper pleasure yet to come—and then he reared back, pulling himself out of her yearning arms and yanked down the zipper of her khaki walking shorts. Curling his fingers into the loosened waistband, he pulled them, and her panties, down her legs and tossed them onto the bricks.

And then he was looming over her again, one hand slipping under her waist to adjust her position, the other hand pulling at the buttons on his fly. Hana set her heels back onto the edge of the hammock and pushed, helping him scoot her backward until she was lying more fully on the blue futon.

"I'm sorry," he said, panting and on his knees between her legs as he finished unbuttoning his jeans. "I can't wait. I have to have you. I *need* you.

Now—" He pushed frantically at the denim fabric that sheathed his narrow hips. "Before I explode."

"It's all right," she breathed, reaching for him as he lowered himself on top of her. "You don't have to wait. I need you, too. It's all right."

"I don't want to hurt you." He brought his fingers to his mouth, gathering moisture to ease his way. "I won't hurt you," he promised and reached down between their bodies. It wasn't necessary. She was swollen and slick, as ready for him as he was for her. With a savage, guttural cry of triumph and need, he slipped his hands under her hips, holding her still for his possession, and thrust himself home.

Hana arched like a too-slender pole under the weight of a prize bluefin. She moaned as he filled her. Her hips rolled convulsively, pressing upward, undulating between his hands.

Quinn groaned, his fingers biting into her hips to still her, fighting against the very real possibility that it would all be over too soon. She was hot and tight and so incredibly responsive. And he was so damned needy. Too needy to be satisfied with a mere moment of bliss. He didn't want a quick tumble and instant gratification—for either of them. He wanted her soft and wet and screaming with the pleasure he could give her. And he wanted the same searing pleasure for himself.

He took a deep, steadying breath, and then another, struggling to bring his rampaging desires under control. He flexed against her, testing his limits, and then again, harder, rotating his hips as he buried himself to the hilt.

Hana went limp and bit back a deep, guttural groan.

"No. Let it out," he demanded as he began to slide in and out of her, measuring his full length on the downstroke, nearly leaving her on the upstroke. "Let me hear how I make you feel." He braced himself on his elbows again, moving his hands up her body, sliding his forearms under her shoulders. He splayed his fingers along the back of her neck, using his thumbs to tilt her chin up so he could look down into her face. "I need to hear. Tell me how I make you feel."

"You make me feel sexy," she whispered, staring up at him, mesmerized by the fierce desire in his green eyes.

"Yes." It was a plea for more.

"And...and..." She writhed beneath him, her pelvis rolling up to meet each slow, powerful, grinding thrust. "And wild."

"Yes."

"And wanted. Like I've never..." Her hands clenched on his shoulders, her nails digging in, as the feeling inside her built, spiraling higher and tighter and hotter, like an ancient island volcano about to erupt. She gasped. "Like I've never been wanted before."

"Yes."

"And I...I..." She cried out, a deep, ragged sound of satisfaction and unbearable pleasure as he pushed her over the top.

"*Yes!*" His hands tightened on her shoulders and his buttocks clenched, pressing downward, holding her hips with the weight of his body until she stopped bucking beneath him.

He soothed her then, moving his trembling hands up to her face, brushing back the wisps and strands of long black hair that clung to her damp cheeks so he could kiss her. He took his sweet time about it, pressing his lips to her flushed cheeks and her eyelids and, finally, her mouth, giving her long, hot, tender kisses that drugged her senses and turned her bones to water, praising her warmth and responsiveness with husky whispers. And then, when she was calm except for an occasional shuddering sigh, he wrapped his arms around her and began to move again.

He started gently but in seconds his thrusts were hard and fast and furious, setting the hammock to swaying beneath them, causing the old ropes to creak out a counterpoint rhythm to their ecstasy. Hana could feel the hunger and urgency in him, the need vibrating through his body like an electric current. It sparked her own needs—the ones she thought had just been satisfied—and she gasped, clinging to him for dear life as she answered the fierce, driving motion of his hips with her own. Her arms were tight around his neck. Her ankles were locked at the small of his back. Her mouth was pressed against the damp, fevered skin of his shoulder in a vain attempt to muffle the primitive, female cries she couldn't contain.

She reached her second climax in moments, tumbling into it, her body arching, straining, slick with sweat against his. And still they pounded at each other. She shrieked and sank her teeth into his shoulder when the third climax hit her; something primitive was driving her to try to claim him as completely as he was claiming her.

Quinn's big body spasmed and stiffened, his arms tightening even more around her as his own release ripped through him. It seemed to go on forever, holding him suspended above her until every last drop of passion had been wrung from his body. Then he groaned like a man mortally wounded and collapsed onto her softness—spent, replete, sated and, for the first time since the earthquake, truly at peace.

Hana lay beneath him, stunned and panting, overwhelmed by the storm that had shaken them both. Where had all that emotion come from? That astonishing need? That furious drive to merge themselves into one being, for however briefly? She'd never before climaxed so many times, so quickly, and with such force; and she wondered, uneasily, if her intense physical response was connected to an equally intense emotional one. It was a scary thought. But wonderful, too. Just like the man who lay gasping for breath in her arms.

She stroked his back with shaky hands, unconsciously striving to comfort them both, and uncrossed her ankles, deliberately loosening the death grip she had around his waist. Her heels slid over the curve of his tightly muscled backside, the soles of her feet coming to rest on the futon on either side of his hips. She felt the denim fabric of his jeans rub against the insides of her thighs as she moved her legs. It made her smile; he'd been in such a hurry he hadn't even gotten his pants all the way off. And she was still wearing her blouse.

She sighed, remembering the way his mouth had felt on her nipple the other morning, and then caught herself wondering if he'd take the time to caress her breasts that way the next time. The thought made her squirm, and if she hadn't already been flushed from his lovemaking, she would have blushed at her own wantonness; there she was, still reeling from the aftereffects of the most powerful sexual experience of her life, and she was already thinking about the next time!

"I'm sorry," he said into her neck. "I'm too heavy for you." He gathered himself to move off her.

"No." Hana's arms tightened. "You're fine right where you are."

"You won't feel that way if I fall asleep on you."

Yes, I will, she thought, but she loosened her arms and let him go.

He pushed himself up, grunting as he rolled to the side.

Hana came up on her elbow, concern pulling her brows together in a frown. "I forgot about your ribs."

His teeth flashed in a satisfied grin. "So did I."

She reached out and touched the fading bruise on his side. "Are you in pain?"

The grin widened. "Not anymore."

"Then you *were* in pain." She sat up, drawing her knees under her as she rose to bend over him. Her fingers probed his side. "I should have known better than to let you exert yourself like that. If we've made your injuries worse, I—"

"Hana." Laughing, he caught her hands in his to still their investigation of his rib cage. "Hana, quit playing doctor for a minute and listen to me. It wasn't my ribs I meant when I said I wasn't in pain anymore," he said when she turned her head to look at him. "It was a rather more, ah, masculine part of my anatomy I was referring to."

Hana shifted her gaze to the portion of his anatomy in question. "Oh."

"It's the first time it's been soft since I woke up with my head on your breasts."

"Oh."

"But I don't think it's going to stay that way for very long."

"Oh?"

"Not long at all." Letting go of one of her hands, he reached up and curled his fingers around the thick black braid hanging over her shoulder. "You have a powerful effect on me, Hana Jamieson," he said, pulling her head down until she was close enough for his lips to brush hers when he spoke. "Damned powerful."

"Is that good?"

"It sure as hell *feels* good." It felt almost too good—better than it had ever felt before, with anyone else. And not just physically, but emotionally, as well. He pushed her hand, the one he still held pressed against his ribs, downward, to avoid having to think about how good it felt. "How's it feel to you?"

She curled her fingers around him. "Powerful," she said, smiling when he groaned against her lips. It was heady stuff, being able to affect him this way. *Powerful*, as he'd said, and moving, and incredibly exciting. She opened her mouth to the tongue licking at her lips and gave in to the feeling.

He lay acquiescent beneath her for a long, delicious moment or two, relishing the sweet aggression in her lips and the hand caressing the growing hardness between his legs. And then he rolled over on top of her, trapping her hand between them, and took control.

He intended to savor her this time, to take her slowly, with all the care and finesse she deserved. He'd been like a bull the last time, so maddened by her taste and scent, so crazed with desire, so needy, that he'd skipped a lot of the pleasures to be had. He wasn't going to skip a single, solitary thing on *this* journey to ecstasy, he promised himself. Not a thing.

He kicked out of his jeans, leaving them in a tangle under the hammock, and then proceeded to peel her out of her blouse. Unknowingly fulfilling her unspoken fantasy, he released each button with maddening slowness, tasting each inch of flesh revealed, lavishing it with teasing strokes of his tongue and minute attention to detail.

It made her sigh when he ran his lips along her collarbone. It made her squirm when he plumped her small breasts in his hands and flicked his tongue in the cleavage he'd created. It made her clench her fingers in his hair when he nibbled his way around her tight little nut-brown areolas. It made her moan when he took her nipple into his mouth and rolled it between his teeth. It made her shiver when he used the ends of her own hair to retrace the path his mouth had taken.

He used what he learned on the rest of her body; dragging his tongue down the insides of her arms and across her palms; raising gooseflesh along her ribs with the ends of her hair; drawing wet little circles around each hipbone; nibbling at her fingertips and the flat skin of her quivering stomach and the backs of her knees; gorging himself on the luscious flesh of her thighs—and higher. He paid a connoisseur's attention to every detail on his sensual journey, cataloging and remembering each heated response she gave him. *This* made her writhe. *This* made her breath catch in her throat. *This* made her groan and arch against him in voluptuous supplication.

When he lifted her hips with his hands to enter her for the second time, she was soft and pliant and utterly receptive to whatever he wanted. Her eyes, lambent with helpless desire, were only half open as she gazed up at him. Her lips were parted, as if ready for his kiss. Her skin was flushed and damp. Her long black hair was unbraided and spread out behind her head, trailing over the edge of the hammock to the bricks of the lanai. The sight of her, so open and ready, touched something half savage in him when he slipped into her clinging warmth—some primal instinct he hadn't even known he had until that moment. He tried to go slow this time, but he couldn't. The need to claim her, to somehow mark her as his while she was so completely vulnerable to him, was too great.

The hammock was swinging wildly again when they both cried out their satisfaction and collapsed into each other's arms. Quinn drew a deep, shuddering breath and rolled to the side to relieve her of his weight; his arms were locked tightly around her, cradling her to him as if he would never let her go; his lips were pressed against the tumbled hair at her temple. He closed his eyes and slept, feeling like more of a man than he'd ever felt in his life.

THEY AWAKENED in the middle of the night, Hana shivering slightly as she snuggled into Quinn in an unconscious effort to avoid the cooling breeze coming in off the ocean. Quinn roused himself and carried her to her bed, fully intending to leave her alone and let her go back to sleep. But she looked so enticing lying there on the cool white sheets, her long black hair tangled around her lithe body, her lips rosy and kiss-swollen, her eyes drowsy from sex and sleep, that he lingered too long. She smiled up at him and held out her arms, and he was lost.

The loving was sweet this time, and tender; the climb to completion slow and steady; the explosion, when it came, a muffled burst of fireworks rather than a volcano's roar. She cuddled against him when it was over, as trusting and sweet as a beloved child, and was asleep before the last shimmers of her climax had completely faded away.

Quinn held her, staring up at the ceiling while he told himself he'd accomplished what he'd set out to do. The last thing Dr. Hana Jamieson would feel for him now was pity. She might hate him, later, when he left her like he'd left all the others over the past year, but she wouldn't pity him. He wondered why that thought didn't give him as much satisfaction as it should have; why he wasn't feeling the unalloyed triumph and satisfaction of a job well-done—"Another one bites the dust"; wasn't that how the song went?—instead of like a prize heel. Either way, heel or hero, it was time for him to get up and leave.

But he didn't. *Couldn't.* Telling himself he would get up in just a minute, that he'd definitely get himself up and out of her bed before she woke up, he wrapped his arms more tightly around Hana Jamieson and went back to sleep.

He lay in the dark, rigid with fear and shame, his arms tight around the child he'd done nothing to save. He couldn't see a thing in the all-consuming blackness. Could barely breathe for the choking dust. Couldn't even feel his legs. But every noise echoed through his head like cannon fire.

"Be quiet," he pleaded with the men who were coming to dig them out. "For God's sake, be quiet."

Didn't they know that one loud noise at just the right frequency could bring it all down around their ears?

He lay there, trapped, sweat pouring off him, listening to the far-off whine of a siren and the sounds of pickaxes and the terrified cries of other victims, and waited for it to come crashing down and crush him to death. He could hear someone shouting orders somewhere above him. Someone else, farther away, was screaming.

"My baby. My baby. Oh, my God, someone save my baby!"

The voice went on and on, high-pitched and hysterical, even when the words ceased to make any sense.

Quinn wondered if the child she was screaming for was the one in his arms. He wondered how much longer he had to live. He wondered if it hurt to die. He wondered if he'd messed himself and they would all know how afraid he'd been. The tears, uncontrollable, sham-

*ing, damning, began to slide down his cheeks, mixing
with the blood and the sweat. He began to panic.*

"Can't breathe. Can't breathe," *he moaned, thrashing around in what little space was available to him, his
arms still tight around the child in his arms.* "Dark,
pressing down. I can't breathe!"

"Mike. Mike, wake up." Hana struggled against
the hard arms that bound her, finally succeeding
in getting a hand free. She reached up and laid it
against his cheek. It was clammy and wet beneath
her palm. "Wake up. You're dreaming." His arms
loosened slightly, enough for her to wriggle up
and cup his face between her hands.

His eyes were wide open, staring in horror and
fear, but he couldn't see her. The tears flowing
down his cheeks nearly tore her heart out. The an-
guish on his face made her soul ache for him.
"Come on, Mike. Wake up," she said frantically,
shaking him a little. "Wake up. It's only a dream.
Wake up."

He blinked, his eyelids flickering as he tried to
focus on her face. "Hana?" he said hesitantly, his
voice thick with residual fear and tears. "Hana?"

"Yes, it's me. It's Hana."

His arms went around her again and he buried
his face in her breasts. "Oh, God, Hana!"

She held him close, rocking him as gently as if
he were a child. "I know," she crooned, stroking
his head. "I know, baby. But it was just a bad
dream, that's all. Just a bad dream."

"No," he said into her breast. "No, it wasn't just
a dream." He angled his head to look up at her,
agony in every line of his face. "We were

trapped.... Tons of mortar and brick on top of us...
And it was dark. So damned dark. People were
screaming. And crying." He ducked his head into
her breast again, ashamed for her to see his tears,
ashamed for her to hear what he couldn't seem to
keep from telling her, yet strangely determined to
tell her everything. "*I* was crying."

"It's all right, Mike," Hana soothed. She
smoothed his sweat-damp hair with her palm.
"Everybody cries sometime. It's all right."

"It isn't all right!" he insisted. "It'll never be all
right!"

"Why won't it be all right?"

"Because she died, Hana." He spoke the words
haltingly, as if every damning syllable was
wrenched up from some wretched place deep in
his soul. "She died in my arms and I didn't do a
thing to save her."

"Who died, Mike?"

"Her name was Maria. Maria Elena Santos."
His voice was bleak. "She was six years old."

Hana held him tighter, as if her arms could
somehow take away his pain. "How did she die?"

"I killed her."

"No." Hana clenched her fingers in his hair and
turned his face back up to hers. "No, I don't believe that, Mike," she said fiercely. "I *won't* believe
it. You didn't kill her. You couldn't have."

"I didn't save her, either. I was supposed to
save her." His voice was rough and full of self-
loathing. "She was counting on me to save her and
I didn't."

"But you tried," Hana said, knowing it was
true. Knowing he would have tried with the last

breath in his body to save any child—any *person*—who needed to be saved. That he was still suffering so horribly over his failure to do so was proof enough of that. "You tried to save her, but the aftershock brought the building down on you, didn't it?" she asked. But it wasn't really a question. She knew, now, what had happened. *You recall that last big quake in California? The one about eighteen months ago? I was a fire fighter. I was inside a partially collapsed building when the first aftershocks hit.* And he'd been inside because he'd been trying to rescue a child. "You can't be blamed for an act of God, Mike."

"It wasn't an act of God, dammit!" He pulled away from her and sat up, his hands clenched into white-knuckled fists, his shoulders hunched and tense, as if he expected to be struck. Without looking at her, he told her what he'd never told another person, not even the department psychiatrist. He didn't know why he told her, except that it was a night for strong emotions. For honesty. And he'd been carrying it around inside him for so long. So damned long. And because he couldn't *not* tell her.

"It was an act of cowardice," he said, staring down at his fisted hands. "I froze, Hana. I lay there, frozen with fear, and a child died!" The expression on his face said he was waiting for her to scorn and revile him for his failure—as he scorned and reviled himself.

"Being afraid isn't a sin."

"It is when other people die because of it."

"Not even then." She reached out and touched

his shoulder. "Not if you've done everything you can. Not if you've already risked your life."

He shook off her touch and looked away, furious and ashamed. "But she *died*. Don't you understand? She died in my arms because I was too scared to do my job."

Hana came up to her knees and reached out, cupping his face between her hands, making him look at her. "What would you have done differently?" she demanded softly. "No, don't turn away." Her fingers tightened to keep him where he was. "Look at me, Mike, and tell me. What *could* you have done differently?"

It was a question he'd asked himself a million times and he still didn't have an answer for it. But that didn't make what had happened easier to bear. He *should* have done something differently.

"You were trapped, just like she was, weren't you?" she said, her eyes burning with tears at the thought. "You were helpless, just like she was. And you were there because you were brave enough and selfless enough to go into that hellhole after her in the first place. And when the building collapsed on top of you, you were afraid. *Anyone* would have been afraid, Mike. *Anyone.* Fear doesn't make you a coward," she said, willing him to believe it. "It only makes you human."

He tried to turn his head away, knowing that not *"anyone"* would have failed because of that fear.

"No, listen to me," she insisted, refusing to let him go, sensing, somehow, that if she lost him now, he would be lost forever. "All of us are afraid sometime, don't you know that?" she said earnestly. "You're not the only one who's been afraid in a life-and-death situation, Mike. And you're not the only one who's ever felt responsible for someone else's death. I've had two patients die in my arms." The tears in her eyes spilled over as she spoke, the memories of those two times as clear in her mind as if they'd happened that morning. "One was a thirty-four-year-old cancer patient with a husband and two kids. The other was a three-year-old drowning victim. And nothing I did—*nothing*—was good enough to save either of them."

"Don't cry, Hana." Quinn reached out, using his thumbs to wipe at the tears that flowed down her cheeks. When that didn't stop them, he wrapped his arms around her and pulled her against his chest. Her arms went around his neck and he sighed, burying his face in the soft place between her shoulder and neck. They knelt there, on the bed, rocking slowly back and forth, comforting each other, grieving for each other, healing each other. "Don't cry." His voice sounded weary and rough, thick with his own tears. "I can't stand to hear you cry."

She sniffled into his neck. "I'm sorry. I didn't mean to cry. I don't know why I'm crying."

"No, don't be sorry." He cupped her head between his hands and turned her face up to his. "Don't be sorry," he said, and kissed her softly— on her cheeks, on her eyelids, on her trembling mouth.

They sank down onto the bed, still locked in each other's arms, instinctively seeking to heal each other with the awesome power of the human touch. Their passion surfaced slowly, inexorably superseding the pain as the one emotion transmuted into the other, building gradually between them until it culminated in bursts of elation and ecstasy.

Hana fell asleep feeling cleansed and cherished and loved.

And Quinn was gone when she woke up the next morning.

7

QUINN TRIED TO TELL himself that what he felt was just plain embarrassment, pure and simple. But it wasn't. Oh, he felt like a prize jackass, all right, blubbering all over Hana like he had, showing her what a "sensitive" guy he was when he'd always felt that "sensitive" was just a polite word for wimp. Or loser.

But, then, wasn't that what he was? A loser? Hadn't he, the Mighty Michael Quinn—and what a joke *that* was!—lost everything in the world that mattered to him? The job he'd been born to do? His friends? His self-respect? And Goddammit all to hell, the only woman he'd ever loved?

Because that's what sweet little Dr. Hana Jamieson had become. Somehow, between the time she'd looked down her elegant nose at him and those glorious, gut-wrenching hours he'd spent in her arms, he'd fallen ass-end-over-teakettle in love with her. And it was a foregone conclusion that he was going to lose her. If she didn't push him away, now that she knew the terrible truth about him, he'd end up running. Just like he'd been doing for the past year. Because how long could he bear to look into her eyes, knowing that she knew he was something less than a real man?

Hell, he was running already. Why else would

he be in a bar at ten o'clock in the morning, intent on getting roaring, stinking drunk?

He rapped his empty glass on the wooden counter. "Another beer down here," he said when Bennie looked up from the receipts he was totaling. "And bring a shot with it. Bourbon."

"You haven't paid me for the first two yet."

"Run a tab."

Bennie shook his head. "You already owe me for damages."

"I'm good for it."

"You'd better be."

Quinn half rose from his barstool, more than ready to take offense. He was spoiling for a fight. With anyone. Over anything. A good rousing, bloody brawl was the only thing that would make the awful feelings of helplessness and self-disgust disappear.

Bennie waved him back down and snagged a clean beer mug off the rack behind the bar. "Settle down, Quinn. I'm not going to trade punches with you. Not over the price of a beer." He pulled on a spigot, sending the golden liquid foaming into the glass. "Over Hana, now, that's a different story. I meant what I said about you hurting her." He placed the glass in front of Quinn, deliberately neglecting to add the shot of bourbon. "Is she why you're in here trying to drink yourself into a stupor?" he asked, giving Quinn a hard look. "Did you hurt her?"

"Not yet," Quinn said, although he was afraid he had. He narrowed his eyes menacingly, giving the other man a hard look back. "Not that it's any of your business."

"What happens on this island is everybody's business, sooner or later," Bennie countered easily. "And, like I said, Hana is my cousin."

"She doesn't look Chinese."

Bennie Chu shrugged. "We share a great-grandmother on her mother's side. The rest of her ancestors are English and French."

Quinn grunted and took a swallow of beer. "Not much of a relationship for you to go poking your nose into her personal business."

"Enough for Paradise." Bennie leaned a companionable elbow on the bar. "So, you running scared or did she finally realize you weren't really wounded and have the good sense to throw you out before you caused her any real trouble?"

Quinn cocked an eyebrow as he lifted his glass to his lips for another long drink, wondering how in hell the bartender had pegged him so well in such a short time.

"Lot of drifters pass through here," Bennie said, as if Quinn had asked the question aloud. "Guys on their way to nowhere, from nowhere. And they've all got the same look about them. Desperate and restless. You had that look all over you."

"Had?"

"You still look kind of desperate." Bennie grinned with a sort of evil enjoyment. "A *lot* desperate, actually. But the lost, restless look is gone." He leaned in closer, considering the face of the man across from him. "I'd say you're a man who's found a woman he might like to settle down with on a permanent basis, and it's got you scared spitless. But hopeful, too." He nodded. "A good woman'll do that to a man. And Hana's a damned good woman."

"Who said anything about Hana?"

Bennie's mouth quirked up at one corner and he shook his head, giving Quinn a look that said, *Don't be more stupid than you can help.*

"All right, so Hana's got something to do with it."

Bennie snorted. "From where I'm standing, I'd say Hana's got everything to do with it."

Quinn scowled and buried his nose in his glass. He didn't like the thought that he could be read so easily—and by some joker he barely knew.

"Let me give you a word of advice about Hana," Bennie said. He waited until Quinn looked up from his beer. "She probably told you her old man was the doctor here on Paradise for a lot of years. What she probably didn't tell you was that he was also a drunk. Real genteellike at first, but after her mother died he turned sloppy. Used to get all weepy when he'd had a few, crying all over anyone who'd listen to what a hard life he'd had and how unfair it all was. Hana was real understanding for a sixteen-year-old girl. She said it was a disease and he couldn't help it. Then she'd take him home and put him to bed and take care of any of his patients that she could the next day. He died of cirrhosis when she was in her third year of med school in the States." He nodded at the beer in front of Quinn. "Hana can't stand the smell of alcohol."

"So, why are you telling me this?"

"Not because I like you, that's for damn sure," Bennie said, although that wasn't precisely true.

Quinn had stood up to Big Louie, and he'd fought fair for as long as he could; that said a lot about his character. And Hana had pretty good instincts about people, despite her tendency to give too many of them a second chance. On the basis of that, Bennie was willing to reserve judgment.

"A blind man could see that Hana likes you, though." Bennie grunted. "More than likes you, from what I can see. If you screw up the courage to stick around for a while, she's going to get involved with you, sure as hell. And being involved with a drunk would hurt her more than she could stand."

Quinn looked down at the half-finished beer in front of him. How much did he want it? How much did he need it compared to how much he needed Hana?

He'd bared his soul to her, telling her his deepest, darkest secret, the thing he'd never told another person, and she hadn't turned away from him. She still might, but...was it likely? Would the woman who'd held him in her arms and loved him so sweetly and so ardently *after* he'd exposed his shameful secret to her, turn away from him later because of that secret?

Hana wouldn't.

Because Hana understood. *"I've had two patients die in my arms,"* she'd said. *"And nothing I did was good enough to save either of them."*

And Hana forgave. Or why else had she let him love her after his desperate confession? And why else had she loved him back?

Sitting there, staring into his beer, Quinn came to the conclusion that Hana's understanding and

forgiveness might—just *might*—make it possible
for him to begin to understand himself, the way
the department shrink had said it was so important that he do. He began to hope that Hana's
sweet and generous spirit might actually help to
make him feel whole again.

Weighed against all that, was *anything* worth
the risk of losing her? Assuming, of course, he
thought wryly, that he hadn't lost her already
with all his stupid, macho posturing. He wasn't
worried about the drinking—he could stop that
any time he wanted—but the thought that Hana
might have been put off by his swaggering, aren't-
I-irresistible routine suddenly had him shaking in
his shoes.

Quinn reached out and, very deliberately,
pushed his beer away, realizing as he did it that
he'd just made an irrevocable, life-altering decision. "Thanks," he said to Bennie as he rose from
the barstool. "I owe you one."

"You owe me a lot more than 'one,'" Bennie
called after him as he walked out of the bar.

But Quinn didn't look back. He had much more
important things on his mind.

HANA DIDN'T CRY WHEN she woke up alone. She
wasn't even really surprised. She'd known before
she'd let him into her life that he was a drifter, a
love-'em-and-leave-'em lady-killer, a brawler and,
worst of all, a borderline drunk. She'd seen him in
action. But it didn't seem to make any difference,
because she'd also seen the pain he was trying so
hard to hide beneath all that renegade behavior,
and she'd been deeply, unbearably touched.

Maybe because she'd hidden a lot of pain in her own life and she knew how it felt. Maybe because she could see the wounded, wonderful man under the lawless rogue. Or maybe, as Bennie had told her countless times, just because she thought it was her duty to try and heal every lost soul who came to her door.

Bennie would also say she'd taken a stupid chance with her life with this lost soul. *And maybe I have,* she thought, placing a hand on her stomach. But she didn't really think so. Though neither of them had used anything last night—the hunger and the need had left little room for thought of anything else—it wasn't her fertile period and conception was highly unlikely. But even if it had been, she realized, she still wouldn't have done things any differently.

She'd still have welcomed him into her arms and her heart, no matter what the reason, and knowing full well that he was bound to leave her, sooner or later.

She just hadn't thought it would be this soon.

And without a goodbye.

The lack of that goodbye hurt, more than she'd ever have thought possible, but there was nothing she could do about it except cry. And crying would only make her eyes red and her chest hurt; it wouldn't change anything, or make her feel any better. Only work would do that. So she swallowed her tears and dove into her work, burying her pain in the problems of other people—as she had always done.

She was in her cramped little office, making

some notes on the final patient of the day, when she heard a shout from her receptionist.

"Doctor Hana. Doctor Hana, come quick!"

She came out of her office at a fast lope, picturing blood and body parts all over her clinic. "What is it, Kim?"

"Look! No. There!" Kim grabbed Hana and turned her around. "Out the window." She pointed over Hana's shoulder. "There."

It was a pretty little sloop, about twenty-five feet long from bow to stern, and as slick as spit. Its hull was gleaming white, trimmed with pale blue. Sunlight bounced off well-oiled teak decks and brightly polished brass. Its sails were furled, the low chug of a small auxiliary motor audible over the water as the single man on board maneuvered to set anchor in the narrow crescent of water bordering the even strip of beach behind Hana's house.

No one used that stretch of water to anchor. Hardly big enough to be called a cove, it was more a depression in the shoreline, and shallow to boot. Hana could and had, many times, walked fifteen feet from the shore before getting wet any higher than her thighs, and another ten feet after that before the water came up as far as her neck.

What in the world does he think he's doing?

"*Firestorm*," Kim said, reading the name painted across the boat's stern as it came about. "Isn't that the sloop that was anchored over in John's Cove? The one that belongs to that hunk you have staying with you?"

"He isn't 'staying' with me," Hana said. "He was a patient in the clinic. And I..." She swallowed the lump in her throat. "I discharged him this morning."

"Well, it looks like he's back. I wonder why."

Hana wondered, too. Did he want to say a proper goodbye before he pointed that pretty little sloop toward the horizon and sailed out of her life for good? Did he want to pay her for her services? Did he want to take her to bed again before he left? And—oh, God—would she let him?

"He's gone over the side," Kim said, as if Hana couldn't see that perfectly well for herself. "He's coming this way."

Hana took a deep breath and squared her shoulders under the white lab coat she wore, telling herself not to read anything more into it than there was, telling herself not to hope. "I guess we'd better go see what he wants."

She stepped out onto the lanai, halting at the edge of the bricks where they gave way to the fine white sand of the beach and waited for him to come to her. He was bare-chested again—still—water glistening on his wide torso and rolling down his washboard belly to the soaked denim that rode low on his hips. He came effortlessly through the water, striding toward the beach like Neptune come to life.

"God, what a body," Kim breathed, unconsciously paraphrasing Hana's pregnant patient of the day before, as well as probably every other woman Quinn had ever crossed paths with.

He halted in front of them, his bare brown feet coated with sand, his wet jeans clinging to every masculine contour of his lower body, sunlight sparkling in the drops of water rolling down his chest. "Hana," he said. His tone made it more a question than a statement of her name.

She looked up at him, blinking back tears, and hoped he couldn't see the pleading and the pain in her eyes.

He reached out and touched her cheek with gentle fingertips, hesitantly and so very, very lightly, uncertain of her response or his welcome, knowing only that he had to try. If she wouldn't have him, well... If she wouldn't have him, he'd promised himself that he'd sail out of her life and never set foot on Paradise again. It was a promise he meant to keep but one he desperately hoped he wouldn't have to; leaving her would surely kill him, putting the final nail in the coffin he'd been building for himself since the earthquake. But, then, he guessed he'd probably want to die if she turned him away. "Hana, I..." His glance flickered over to the young woman standing at Hana's side with her mouth hanging open.

"Kim, we'd like to be alone, please," Hana said without taking her eyes off Quinn's face. She didn't want to miss any nuance of his expression, any flicker of emotion that might tell her what he was going to say so she could prepare herself before he said it.

Neither of them watched as the young woman moved away. Neither of them could have said if she did or not. Their world had narrowed to just two people, and they had eyes only for each other.

Emboldened by her passive acceptance of his presence, Quinn allowed his hesitant touch to become a tender caress. He cupped her cheek in his palm, looking down at her with his heart in his eyes. He'd had a whole speech planned—pretty words to make her want him, measured words to convince her that he could change for her sake. But only one thing really mattered: "Hana, I want to stay."

"Stay?"

"Here. In Paradise. With you."

Hana didn't even think about it. She knew she should have, that there were problems, that he would probably cause her untold pain and grief, but it didn't matter. Nothing mattered except that he had come back. And he wanted to stay. Her lips curved upward in a tremulous smile.

"Yes," she said simply, exactly the way she'd said it last night, just before she'd offered him her lips—and her love.

Quinn was filled with awe and thanksgiving. She could have made him suffer—he deserved to suffer for the callous way he'd treated her—but she smiled up at him instead, giving him his heart's desire without questions or accusations. "Aren't you even going to ask me why?"

"I don't care why."

His other hand came up and he cradled her face in his hands, holding her as if she were something precious and rare. Hana lifted her own hands and wrapped them around his wrists. "You don't care that I love you?" he whispered.

"Do you?"

"You know I do."

Yes, she thought. *I know. Now.* Standing there, looking up into his fierce, loving green eyes, she didn't know how she could ever have doubted it.

"I don't know how it happened," he said softly,

with a new lover's eagerness to tell his beloved all the details of his wondrous feelings for her. "Or when, exactly. I think it was when you came into Bennie's and turned up your nose at me for being such a disgusting pig."

"I never thought you were disgusting."

"I know I'm no bargain, Hana. I haven't got a job or much of a future. My psyche's all twisted up in knots most of the time. I've been drinking too much and I'll probably make you cry twice a day. But I can get a job and I've stopped drinking altogether and we can make a new future. And, Hana, I love you."

"Oh, Mike," she breathed, hearing only the most important part of his declaration. "Oh, Mike, I love you, too."

He leaned closer to her, his hands still on her face, and she came up on tiptoe, levering herself with her hands on his wrists. Their lips touched, softly, reverently, with hope and joy and painful longing.

"Oh, Hana," he said. And then he gave a shout of laughter and flung his arms around her hips, grabbing her up against him so that her feet came off the ground.

Hana clutched his shoulders and laughed, too, from pure happiness as he whirled them around and around.

He stumbled after a turn or two, losing his balance on the uneven surface of the beach. Hana shrieked as they went down. They rolled in the warm sand like children, her in her white lab coat and him soaking wet, laughing as the sand clung to them and they clung to each other. And then, abruptly, their eyes met and locked, and they stopped laughing.

"I love you, Hana Jamieson. More than you'll ever know."

"I know," she said, with complete conviction in her voice as she gazed up at him. "I love you, too."

"I'll do my best to be worthy of you."

"No." She lifted her hand and covered his lips with her fingertips. "No, don't say that. You don't have to do your best to be worthy of anyone. You *are* worthy, just by being you."

"Oh, Hana," he said again and lowered his head to kiss her.

8

THEY SPENT THE NEXT TWO weeks strengthening the ties that bound them to each other, banishing everyone from their newly blissful world except the people they absolutely had to see—Hana's patients and Kim; the various shopkeepers and merchants necessary to keep them stocked with the material necessities of life; and Bennie the one time he dropped by to visit and then left after only ten minutes because it was obvious that he was *de trop*.

Quinn swam in the warm waters outside Hana's back door when she was busy practicing her profession; he ran the white sand beaches for miles, until his lungs burned and his legs ached, exorcising a year's worth of alcohol and self-neglect from his system. He fed an honorable man's basic need to contribute to the well-being and security of his beloved by doing odd jobs around the house and clinic.

And he loved Hana into delighted insensibility whenever she got close enough to touch, reinforcing and affirming one of the most basic bonds of all with his hands and his lips and his powerful body. And when their loving was over, when their heartbeats slowed and the passion cooled to a simmer, they lay in each other's arms, flushed and damp and relishing their closeness, and talked. About everything.

"As FAR BACK AS I CAN remember, Dad drank more than most people," Hana said. She was sprawled naked on top of Quinn on the deck of the *Firestorm* as it rocked at anchor in front of her clinic. Her legs were between his, her breasts against his bare belly, her chin resting on the backs of the hands she'd laid atop his breastbone. "But before my mother died I can't ever remember seeing him drunk. Not falling-down, sloppy drunk. I knew how much he'd loved and depended on my mother—he always said she was his salvation and his whole reason for living—so I tried to understand his pain and make excuses for him, but..." She shrugged and smiled a bit wistfully. "Sixteen-year-old girls aren't known for their understanding."

"You were," Quinn said, wondering if he'd eventually have ended up like Hana's father. "Bennie told me how you used to take care of your father. And how you defended him by telling everyone that his alcoholism was a sickness and he couldn't help it. That sounds pretty understanding to me."

"I know what it *sounds* like, but..." She pulled one hand out from under her chin and plucked at Quinn's chest hairs. "It was all a cover-up," she said softly, not looking at him.

"A cover-up?"

"Inside, I was ashamed of him," she admitted, telling him what she'd never told anyone else. "I knew he was suffering from a disease, but I still thought he should be able to overcome his suffering and I... Well, I hated him sometimes, for what he'd turned into." She said the words quickly, as if she was afraid Quinn would fault her for them. "I hated him because he couldn't stop wallowing in his own grief long enough to think about mine. And because he never seemed to think about what his drinking did to me."

"And you hated *yourself* for feeling that way," Quinn said with the conviction of a man who'd had more than his share of experience with the same feeling.

"Yes."

Quinn covered the slender hand plucking at his chest hairs, pressing it flat against him with his hand. "You've got to know what you felt wasn't unusual under the circumstances. It would have been unusual if you *hadn't* hated him sometimes."

"Oh, I know," Hana said. "Intellectually, I know. I've read the textbooks and the case studies. But emotionally well..." She flicked a nervous glance at her lover, wondering how he'd take her next statement. "Every time I smell alcohol on someone's breath I feel like that sixteen-year-old girl who felt guilty because she hated her father for something he couldn't help."

Quinn's chest lifted on a sigh of regret. "And the first time I kissed you I was reeking of it."

"Yes."

"And it made you think of your father and how you hated what he was."

She bit her lip but answered honestly. "Yes."

There was a long beat of silence as Quinn considered all the ramifications of that. "And now you're wondering if some day I'm going to turn into a slobbering drunk and make you just as miserable as he did, despite what I said about quitting."

Hana thought of denying it. It wasn't what she thought, not exactly, but it was painfully close. She *knew* how hard it was to quit drinking, even for a man as strong-willed as the Mighty Quinn. And he *still* had the occasional beer; not often, true, but occasionally. Which *didn't* mean he was an alcoholic, or even close to it, but—

"Hana?"

She lifted her eyes to his. "Yes," she answered softly, hating to say it but knowing it had to be said. "I sometimes wonder if you'll end up like my father."

"And yet you let me stay," Quinn said, awed. "Why?"

"Bennie would say it's because I'm a sucker for a lost soul."

"And you, Hana?" he asked tensely. "What do you say?"

"I love you," she said simply. "I know it's probably not the smartest thing I've ever done," she added in a rush. "And even though I'm deliriously happy now, I know there's a chance you'll make me miserable later, but I don't seem to care about later. That is, I *do* care, but..." She shrugged helplessly. "I love you."

"Thank God," Quinn said, meaning it with every fiber of his being. "Because I love you, too. More than I'll ever be able to tell you." He sat up as he spoke, pushing Hana to her knees on the oiled deck of the *Firestorm*, and coming up on his own. He cupped her face in his palms. "I promise you right here and now," he said, staring down into her eyes with a fierce, intense light in his, "that I'll never, ever make you miserable, Hana. Not over my drinking. As of right now, that's finished. Kaput. Over."

"You don't have to prom—" Hana began. Her father had promised to quit, time and time again, and she knew how hard such promises were to keep. And how damaging they were when they were broken. She'd rather have him keep drinking than promise and fail, over and over again.

He put his thumbs over her lips. "I know I don't *have* to promise," he said, "but I want to. I need to. And I need you to believe in that promise. I need you to believe in *me*." He brushed at the strands of hair the ocean breeze had blown across her face, tenderly smoothing them back out of her eyes. "Can you do that, Hana? For me? For us?"

"Yes," she said without hesitation, hoping it was true. She wanted to believe. So badly. And, if she couldn't quite trust his promise, she most emphatically trusted him. It would have to be enough. She smiled tremulously. "Yes, I believe you."

"I'll never come to you with booze on my breath like I did those first two times," he said, still serious and intense. "Never."

Hana's smile widened by a sweet, teasing margin. "Will it give you a swelled head if I tell you I don't actually remember smelling alcohol the first time you kissed me? Before, of course, and afterward, but not *while* you were kissing me."

"Yeah?" Quinn's expression lightened, his grin

almost matching hers. "What do you remember about it?"

"I remember being surprised that your lips were so soft," she said, reaching out to place a fingertip against them, "when they look so hard. And I remember feeling the stubble of your beard against the skin around my mouth." She moved closer to him, stretching up from her knees so she could touch her lips to the corner of his. His arms went around her waist as she continued. "And I remember being amazed that you could hold me so tightly and so gently at the same time."

"And what about the second time I kissed you?" he asked, his green eyes beginning to gleam with a familiar light.

She gave him an arch look. "I was asleep."

"No, you were asleep when I kissed your breast. But you were awake by the time I got to your lips."

"So I was," she murmured. "But I seem to remember your mouth on my breast more clearly." She looped her arms around his neck. "Especially the second time."

They were skin to skin now, their bodies touching from chest to knees. "So what do you remember about it?" he demanded.

"The heat," she said, nuzzling his cheek with her lips. "And wishing it would never end, even though I knew it had to."

"Oh, Hana?"

"Hmm?"

"It isn't my head that's swelling."

"No?" She pulled away from him slightly, sliding her hands down to his chest as if to create the little distance needed for her to look down and see exactly what the problem was.

"Do you think you can help me, Doc?"

"Oh, definitely," she said, laughter and mischief in her voice. And then she pushed against his chest, toppling him over the side of the *Firestorm* and into the blue Pacific.

HANA KNELT ON THE BED beside Quinn, tracing the raised welts on his right leg with a gentle fingertip. She could tell by the tenseness of his big body that he'd much rather she would concentrate on some other part of his anatomy, but he lay there, naked and exposed, and let her look.

"How long were you in physical therapy?"

"Almost six months," he said, watching her face for any signs of revulsion. She was a doctor, yes, and she'd probably seen a lot worse, but it wasn't the scars that bothered him so much as what they represented. And what they represented was failure. And cowardice.

"I'm impressed," Hana said, and meant it. "Judging by the extent of these scars, you must have progressed very quickly to have spent only six months in therapy."

"I wanted to get out of that damned hospital as fast as possible." He snorted with exaggerated disgust, not wanting her to know how much the experience had affected him. "All those damned nosy doctors, poking and prodding a person, leaving a man without a shred of dignity or privacy."

Hana slanted him an amused smile. "Present company exempted, of course?"

"Oh, of course," he said, implying that wasn't the case at all.

Hana's smile widened. "Liar," she said, and went back to examining his leg. "The bone came through here, didn't it?" she asked, but it wasn't really a question. "And here." Her eyes misted. "The pain must have been unbearable."

"Not really. They kept me so doped up most of the time, I didn't feel a thing."

Something in his voice alerted her to the meaning beneath the words. "And you wanted to, didn't you?"

"Wanted to what?"

"Feel the pain," she said softly. "You wanted to be punished for what you perceived as your failure."

For a moment he considered denying it—it sounded like a load of self-indulgent psychobabble—but he realized it was true. "Yeah," he said finally. "Yeah, I wanted to feel the pain. It would have...helped."

"That's why you went around getting into all those fights, wasn't it? And why you drank too much, and why you got involved with women you didn't respect. You were punishing yourself."

"Yes, I guess I was," he said haltingly. He realized for the first time that he hadn't been acting like the meanest, baddest, most rotten kid on the block to prove anything about his manhood—or, at least, not completely. Instead, he'd been doing his best to punish himself for being alive when Maria Santos was not. No one else would do it for him, so he'd had to do it himself.

And I was doing a damned good job of it, too, he

thought. So good that he'd probably have managed to get himself killed within a year or two. Eventually, some goon would have knifed him in a bar, or some hooker would have given him a fatal disease, or he'd have fallen off his boat, dead-drunk and unable to save himself.

But then he'd run into Hana—warm, wonderful, understanding, honest Hana—and the fast track to total destruction had suddenly seemed like the wrong road to be on.

"You've punished yourself enough," she said sternly, staring down at him with the fierceness of a mother protecting her young. "I won't allow you to continue to castigate yourself for something that wasn't even your fault. Is that clear?"

"Perfectly," he said, lying through his teeth.

"And you're to think of these scars as the badges of honor they are, and not some hideous symbol of a nonexistent failure."

"All right," he agreed mildly, amused and deeply touched by her passionate advocacy of him, even against his own opinion of himself.

"Because they *are* badges of honor." She bent down to him and touched her lips to the worst of the scars. "Every one of them."

Quinn reached out and pulled her into his arms, wondering if he'd ever reach the point where he could share her high opinion of himself.

"I'VE FIXED EVERY squeaky hinge," Quinn said one evening as they lay together in the hammock, looking up through the lacy palm fronds at the stars. "I've planed every door and window in the place. The plans for the addition to the clinic are complete. I need to go to work."

"You can get everything you need at Matsunaga Lumber," Hana said, her voice lazy with contentment. "And what he doesn't have, I'm sure you can get over on Nirvana."

"No. I mean real work, Hana. A job."

She went very still in his arms, realizing that their days in their own private paradise were about to come to an end. She'd known that reality was going to intrude sometime, as it always did; she just wished it hadn't intruded so soon. "Why can't we just stay the way we are?" she said plaintively, fearing what a world full of everyday temptations and trials would do to them.

"Because I can't continue to live off you like some parasite, that's why."

"You're not living off me," Hana objected. "You contribute your share."

Quinn sighed. He could have been contributing more, monetarily speaking. He had an ever-increasing bank account in the States, the total balance swelling monthly with the disability checks the department insisted on sending him. They said he'd earned it, that he had a right to it, but he knew he hadn't and didn't. It was blood money, "earned" by an act of cowardice, and he refused to touch a penny. Hence, the need for a job.

"Who's going to be paying for those supplies I'm supposed to get over at Matsunaga's?" he asked.

"Well—" Hana squirmed against him, coming up onto her elbow so she could look at him. "I will, but you'll be building my new examining

room and office," she said earnestly. "So that
evens it out. And it is *my* clinic. By rights I should
be paying you to do the work."

"No."

"But—"

"But nothing. I'm not taking money from you,
Hana, and that's that. And you're not buying another load of groceries, either."

She stuck her bottom lip out at him, trying to
tease him out of his seriousness. "That's a very
old-fashioned attitude."

"No, that's the way of the world," he said, refusing to be teased. "A man doesn't take money
from his woman. And he doesn't let her support
him, either. *He* takes care of *her*, if he's any kind of
man at all."

"And you're definitely all man," she purred.

His eyes glinted up at her in the dark. "You're
not going to use sex to change my mind, Doc," he
said sternly, but there was a smile lurking around
the corners of his mouth.

She ran a soft fingertip over his lips. "I can try,
can't I?"

"Oh, sure, you can try." He grinned and nipped
at her fingertip. "By all means, try all you want.
But it isn't going to get you anywhere." He rolled
over, trapping her beneath him in the hammock.
"Except flat on your back, where all you uppity
women belong," he said, and kissed her laughing
protest into silence.

"DO YOU HAVE TO WORK at that hotel?"

"We've gone over this before, Hana. It's the
only job in Paradise that pays a halfway decent

wage. And it's the only thing I know besides fire fighting."

"But it's ruining the island."

"It's *changing* the island. There's a difference."

"Not from where I'm standing."

He put a hand on her shoulder and tilted her chin up with the other, forcing her to look at him. "Hana, be reasonable. Paradise needs jobs. It needs growth and an influx of new money. This new hotel can be the start of that."

"How?" She jerked her chin out of his hand but didn't move away from his touch on her shoulder. If they were going to have a parting of the minds, she wanted to be connected to him on a more basic level. "Those developers are using mostly off-islanders to build it, and they're bringing in most of the supplies, too. How's that going to help the people of Paradise or its economy?"

"The developers are hiring anyone willing to work who knows how to use a hammer—off-islander or not," Quinn countered, moving his hands to the small of her back and interlacing his fingers. "And they're buying as much as they can from Paradise's businesses. It's not their fault there isn't much to buy."

Hana rested her hands on his chest. "And what about the accidents?" she demanded, unwilling to give in. "What about the code violations?"

"Accidents of one kind or another are a fact of life on any major construction site, which you'd know if there'd ever been any major construction on Paradise before. And there haven't been any building-code violations for the simple reason that there isn't any building code to speak of. You told me that yourself, if you'll recall."

"So it's okay if they put up an unsafe building, if they don't break any laws *while* they build it? Is that what you're saying?"

"No, that's not what I'm saying, and you know it. They may not be building their hotel with all the safeguards and the scrupulous attention to detail they'd have to in most cities in the States, but they *are* adhering to at least minimum standards. I wouldn't be working there if they weren't, and neither would anyone else with more than two brain cells to rub together."

Hana stuck her bottom lip out at him.

He grinned and rocked her from side to side. "You don't think they'd take the chance that their new hotel would fall in on a paying customer, do you?"

"Well, no, but..." She twisted a button on the front of his sweat-stained work shirt. "They're ruining the natural environment on the south shore," she said stubbornly. "And if one hotel's successful, what's to stop them from building a dozen more? Two dozen more?"

"The island council, if they'll get off their collective butts and pass some legislation against it." He gave a disgusted snort. "They're as much to blame as the developers for whatever effect the hotel has on Paradise. Maybe more."

"How do you figure that?"

"Because the developers are doing what developers do—developing. It's up to the residents to see that they don't go too far. And, from what I can tell, the island council hasn't done one single, blessed thing to set any limits."

A calculating gleam lit Hana's eyes. "Come to the next council meeting with me and tell them that."

"You tell them that. It's your island."

"It's your island now, too." She paused, looking up at him from under her lashes. "Isn't it?"

"Yes," he said, as if he were just now considering it. *Really* considering it. "Yes, I guess it is."

"Well, then...?"

"I doubt your island council would be willing to listen to anything some broken-down ex-fire-fighter has to say. Especially one who's been on the island less than a month."

"You aren't a 'broken-down' anything," Hana said indignantly. "And, now that you've mentioned it, I might as well tell you that I've... Well, that I've been giving a lot of thought to your ex-profession."

"You have, huh?" he said uneasily, leaning back a bit to peer down at her. He was beginning to recognize that look on her face; it usually portended some brainstorm she'd come up with that included his cooperation, whether he wanted to give it or not. "What kind of thought?"

"Well..." She tilted her head and smiled up at him. "Paradise doesn't have a real fire department and I thought—"

"Now, Hana, we've discussed this." He dropped his hands from her waist and turned away, sudden panic slashing at his insides.

"I know you don't want to go back to work as a full-time fire fighter," Hana said hurriedly. "I'm not suggesting that. I don't think Paradise has the money to pay a full-time fire fighter, anyway. And we don't even have a real fire station. I just thought you might train some of our volunteers, that's all. Honest."

The panic began to recede a bit. She wanted him to organize and train a volunteer fire department. That wasn't so bad. It was, in fact, a far cry from what he'd expected her to come up with when she said she'd been thinking about his ex-profession. He could probably handle training a volunteer force. And it would be a way to get back into the work he loved, if only partway. And he could do it without falling apart at the seams, or revealing his last, most damning weakness to Hana, couldn't he? She knew that he had *been* afraid—in the past, before he'd known her. She didn't know that he was *still* afraid.

She touched his shoulder. "Mike?"

"I'll think about it."

QUINN STROLLED INTO HER almost-completed new office two weeks later with a look of tremendous satisfaction on his handsome face. "I've found us a fire truck."

Hana looked up from the medical file in front of her. "You've found a fire truck? Really?" She half rose from her chair in excitement and then sank back into her seat, tamping her excitement until she had all the facts. "How much is it going to cost?"

"Just shipping. And the island council may not even have to fork over the money for that," he added, thinking of the money that was, even now, accumulating in his Stateside account. What better way to spend it than in funding Hana's dreams of a better Paradise?

"Just shipping costs?" Hana frowned. "It's a steam engine, right?"

"It's about fifteen years old but in perfect condition."

"So, what's the catch?"

"No catch." He sat down in the chair across from her desk. "I remembered an old pal in California. He's got what you might call a passion for helping out the less fortunate members of the firefighting brotherhood. He's been scrounging used equipment and supplies for years, ever since he went on a fact-finding mission in South America and saw the substandard equipment some of the fire fighters in underdeveloped countries have to contend with. Whenever he can get his hands on surplus equipment he gets it to where it will do the most good. I figured Paradise qualifies as underdeveloped, so I called him."

"That's it? You just called him and—voilà! Paradise has a fire truck?"

"Well, there was a little luck involved, too. He'd just run across this particular fire truck a few days ago and hadn't allocated it yet." Quinn leaned back in the chair and crossed a bare ankle over the opposite knee. "He came across a complete field hospital a couple of years ago," he said casually, as if it weren't really important. "One that'd never been used."

"A complete field hospital?"

"Uh-hmm." Quinn pretended not to notice the

avid expression in her eyes. "He even shipped a fully loaded ambulance once."

"How often does a person come across a field hospital?" Hana wanted to know, seeing her dreams of someday having a real hospital, or, at least, a fully stocked clinic on Paradise suddenly a little closer to coming true. "And who do I have to sleep with to get on this guy's list for the next one he finds?"

Quinn grinned at her. "You're sleeping with him."

"Oh, Mike!" Hana jumped up from her chair and flung herself at him. "Oh, Mike!"

He caught her easily, settling her comfortably on his lap in spite of the way she twisted around to wind her arms around his neck. "If you're real nice to me," he said, "I might even ask him to keep an eye out for an X-ray machine. Maybe even one of those ultrasound things that you use on pregnant ladies."

"Oh, I can be real nice," Hana assured him, raining kisses over his face and neck. "Very nice. *Extremely* nice. You have no idea how nice I can be."

He hugged her tight, close to his heart. "Show me," he said.

HANA GOT OUT OF HER VAN, the brown paper sack that Quinn had left on the kitchen table that morning clutched in the fingers of one hand. Her gaze was on the half-finished facade of the newest— and only—hotel complex on Paradise. She had to admit that it wasn't really the skyscraper she'd called it. According to what Mike had told her, it was only going to be six stories tall at its highest point. And she could tell from what had already been done that someone had made an effort to see that it blended into the existing landscape as well as such a large structure could.

It was, she saw as she moved toward it, actually three separate buildings, each a different height, strung together with wide, covered walkways. The location would obviously be very attractively landscaped when it was finished. As few trees as possible had been cut to make way for the buildings and, from the work already under way, Hana could see that even more trees and shrubs were being planted to compensate for what had been cut down.

Maybe—just maybe—it wasn't going to be quite the blight on Paradise that she'd thought it would be. She smiled to herself. *But I'll be damned if I'll admit it*, she thought.

She leaned her head back as she approached the closest structure, her hand tented over her eyes, and peered up the half-finished side in an effort to locate the very person she was least likely to admit her recent change of heart to. She spied him, finally, halfway up a long metal ladder, wearing a yellow hard hat and doing something macho with a power tool.

He'd discarded his shirt, as usual, and his muscled torso gleamed with the sweat of a healthy, hardworking male. His tight buns and long legs were encased in dusty jeans. Scruffed, muddy work-boots were laced around his ankles. A tool belt dangled across his lean hips.

Hana sighed and tilted her head back farther,

unable to look away as she waited for him to finish whatever he was doing. She was probably going to get a crick in her neck, but the view was most definitely worth it. Still, as soon as the power drill whined to a stop, Hana pursed her lips and whistled—a long, low wolf whistle that would have done credit to any self-respecting male chauvinist on any construction crew in the world. "Shake it, baby, shake it!" she hollered, ignoring the other construction workers who turned around to stare.

Quinn obligingly shook his fanny at her.

Hana gave a low catcall and whistled again.

The other construction workers hooted. "Shame on you, Doc Hana!" someone called. But Hana ignored him, too, her eyes on the small tight backside of the man on the ladder.

He turned around and grinned down at her. "I could file a sexual-harassment suit against you for that kind of lewd behavior," he said and began climbing down the ladder.

Hana laughed. "You wanna talk about lewd behavior? I'll tell you about lewd behavior." Her voice lowered to a husky whisper as he closed the distance between them. "There's a certain incident involving the stirrups on my examining table that I'm sure the AMA would frown on if they knew about it."

Quinn gave her a heated look. "It was your examining table," he reminded her.

"Yeah, but it was your idea."

"Well, what can I say?" He dropped lightly to the ground and reached out, wrapping a sweaty arm around her waist, the power drill still clutched in his other as he lowered his lips to her ear. "I'm inventive."

"You certainly are." She snuggled up to him, ignoring both the sweat that glistened on his chest and the interested stares of the other men on the construction site. She reached up to wrap both arms around his neck, despite the brown paper lunch sack in her left hand. "Lucky me," she murmured, and lifted her lips for his kiss.

He shoved the drill into his tool belt like a gunslinger holstering his gun, and wrapped both arms around her waist, lifting her off her feet as he deepened his possession of her mouth.

"Hubba, hubba, Doc!" someone hollered from above them.

"Show her who's boss, Quinn," shouted someone else.

"You two want to knock it off there?" a third man said from behind them, with mock gruffness. "You're disrupting the work force."

"Ignore him," Hana said, sotto voce, but she swung around in her lover's embrace, turning to face the man behind them. She smiled when she recognized a native islander—an older and very well-respected man—under his yellow hard hat. The sight of him altered her opinion of the hotel complex another notch toward acceptance. "Isn't it about time for the lunch whistle?" Hana suggested, holding up the brown paper sack she'd brought.

"Lunch whistle already blew," the man answered, gesturing toward the men who were swarming down the ladders and off the site toward a small, shaded area set up with sawhorse tables and rough plank benches. "While you and lover boy, there, were trying to find each other's tonsils."

"I thought I heard bells," Quinn murmured.

Hana blushed and not-so-discreetly elbowed him in the ribs as he led her away from the half-finished building toward the lunch area.

"Got an extra cold one there?" Quinn called to another construction worker crouched over an open cooler.

"Catch."

Quinn caught it in one hand. "Thanks."

"You want one?" the man asked Hana.

"No, thanks," she said, stiffening slightly in Quinn's embrace.

He looked down at her. "It's nonalcoholic beer," he said, turning the can so that she could see the label. "No booze on a construction site."

Hana instantly felt guilty for her instinctive re-action. "I didn't mean—I wasn't—"

"Yes, you did. But it's all right, honey." He squeezed her lightly, trying not to let her see how hurt he was by her suspicions. "You're entitled to a doubt or two, considering." His teeth flashed in a grin meant to reassure her that there were no hard feelings. "But only one or two."

She stopped him, reaching out to touch his bare forearm as he extended it to pull out the end of a bench. "I trust you, Mike," she said when he turned his head to look at her inquiringly. "Completely. And if you want an occasional beer, fine. Not here, I know," she added when he opened his mouth to answer her. "But other times. When you're at home or on the boat. Wherever." She waved the hand that held their sack lunch. "What I mean is, I know you're not an alcoholic." No alcoholic had ever given up the drug so easily. "You don't have to give up the occasional beer because of me."

"I didn't," Quinn said. "I gave it up because of me."

FLAMES LICKED UP the sides of the wooden structure with the appetite of a savage, untamed beast, waving out the windows as if it were taunting the fire fighters outside. Smoke billowed up in a thick cloud, carrying the smell of ash and soot into the air. The searing heat, more than the sawhorse barriers, kept the crowd a safe distance away.

Quinn settled the strap of his yellow fire hat more firmly under his chin with the tip of his index finger and grinned in satisfaction; the first "live" training exercise of the new Paradise Volunteer Fire Department was under way and, so far, so good.

"Okay, Louie, put your hands here. And here." Quinn demonstrated with the huge nozzle of the new fire hose and then handed it to Paradise's newest volunteer fire-fighter. "Get a good grip—that's it—and brace yourself. When you feel it coming, lean into it and hold on tight."

"Kinda like a woman, huh?"

"*Exactly* like a woman," he said, glancing over at Hana to see if she'd heard the exchange. Her expression told him she had. He smiled at her before turning his attention back to Big Louie. "If you're not ready when the water comes out, it'll knock you flat on your butt," he warned.

"I'll be ready."

Quinn nodded to the men at the water valve. "Let 'er rip."

There was a protesting whine of metal against metal as the valve was released, and then the hose began to move, swelling and twitching as if a live thing were racing through it. Big Louie leaned back, his feet braced wide, as water shot out of the nozzle in his hands with the force of a cannon. He didn't have to alter his stance by so much as a fraction of an inch.

"Ride 'em cowboy," someone hollered, and Louie grinned.

Quinn couldn't help but grin in response. He'd been surprised when his barroom nemesis had signed up as a volunteer fire-fighter, but Big Louie swore he didn't hold a grudge against any man who'd beat him in a fair fight; and since he'd ended up enjoying the services of Angel, anyway, he felt he had even less grounds for resentment. Quinn didn't remember the fight as being quite fair, but he didn't argue. The Paradise Volunteer Fire Department needed all the willing bodies it could get.

"That's great, Louie," Quinn said as he watched the massively built man handle the heavy fire hose as easily as if it were the green plastic garden variety. "Great. Long, slow, sweeping motions. Not too fast. That's it." He watched a few minutes more, then tapped Louie on the shoulder. "Let, ah—" he scanned the volunteers "—Peterson—" he decided "—have a whack at it." He spent a moment explaining the easiest procedure for transferring the hose, then stepped back and let them handle it. If it got loose, well, that was another lesson they needed to learn, anyway.

It felt good, being back in harness again, he thought as he stood back and watched the men perform the maneuvers that, up until now, had only been classroom theory to them. It felt real good.

He'd had a bad moment or two at first, wondering if the crippling fear he'd felt since the accident would come back, once he was actually facing a fire, but it hadn't. He finally realized that it wasn't the fire that brought on the cold sweats; it was the thought of being trapped and helpless, with no way out. He might have learned that lesson back in California, if he'd given himself the chance, but he hadn't gone back on active duty after the accident. He'd been too afraid. Afraid to try. Afraid to fail.

He'd been able to try on Paradise because of Hana. And, if he was being honest with himself, because, on a subconscious level, at least, he must have been aware that there was little chance of him finding himself in a situation that would bring the terror back. Paradise had no high-rises. It had no earthquakes.

That wasn't to say something couldn't still happen; that he would never be trapped in a burning building, for instance. But the risk was minimal, and he could live with it. With luck, he'd never have to face his fear again, never have to find out how big a coward he really was.

He felt a hand at his waist and turned toward the source. "Civilians are supposed to stay behind the barrier," he said to Hana, but he dropped a long arm around her shoulders and pulled her close.

"Is everything all right?"

"Everything's fine. Why?"

Hana shrugged. It wasn't anything she could put her finger on. "You just looked a little pensive standing here all by yourself," she said.

"Just reviewing the troops."

"And you're sure you're all right?"

He gave her a little squeeze. "Couldn't be better," he assured her.

"WHAT COLOR DO YOU THINK I should paint the examining room?" Hana asked as she shuffled through the dazzling array of cardboard color samples spread out on the kitchen table.

"Anything but that puky hospital green," Quinn said without looking up from the schedule he was working out for the fire department. "I hate that color."

"As if I would," Hana said, affronted. "I was thinking either Ivory Blush or Blushing Beige." She held up two oblong cards. "What do you think?"

Quinn barely glanced at them. "Either one."

"Mike." She said it with a petulant edge, making two syllables of it.

He sighed with pretended reluctance and looked up from his schedules to study the color samples she was holding in either hand. "Either one," he said again.

Hana frowned.

"Well, they both look sorta pink to me."

"They both *are* 'sorta' pink," she said, grinning,

and reached across the table to swat him with the card she held. "But which one do you like best?"

"I don't know." He looked back and forth between the two cards and shrugged. "Either—" He bit off the rest of what he was going to say, his teasing grin matching hers. "Aren't they kind of froufrou looking for an examining room?"

"Maybe." She looked down at the cards again. "But most of my patients are women and children, so it's all right. And, anyway, I read in some article that pink has a calming effect on people, which would be good for an examining room." She laid the two cards to one side and began searching for more pinks. "The article said it's being used in some prisons and mental institutions to cut down on the violence."

"Probably turns all the inmates into sweet little fruitcakes."

"Mike Quinn! What a thing to say!"

He was unrepentant. "But probably the truth."

"Ha! What it probably does is reduce testosterone levels."

"Better get rid of those things, then." Quinn reached across the table as if to snatch up all the pink cards, but Hana leaned over, covering them with her outspread hands and forearms. "We don't want anybody's testosterone levels dropping around here, do we?" Quinn said, looking as innocent as he could with a day's growth of beard stubbling his chiseled jaw. "That wouldn't be any fun."

Hana's lips curved up in a very feminine smile. "Your testosterone levels could drop by half and you'd still be more 'fun' than most women could handle."

"But not you, huh?"

"Not me," she said, utterly confident. "I was born to handle you."

Her words had his eyes blazing. "Oh, Hana." He swept the color cards and schedules off the table with his forearm. Reaching across to lift her out of her chair, he dragged her onto her back on the smooth surface, intent on giving her as much as she could "handle" right then and there.

The phone rang, slicing through their rising passion.

"Ignore it," Quinn ordered, his hands already sliding into the waistband of her shorts.

"I can't," she moaned. "It's the clinic number. It could be an emergency."

He levered himself up off the table with a groan. "Don't move," he growled, and reached for the phone himself. "Dr. Jamieson's office," he said, staring at Hana with sensual heat simmering in his green eyes. "What? Yes. Just a minute." He covered the mouthpiece with his hand. "Darlene Kapaua has gone into labor," he said to Hana.

She sprang off the table and grabbed the phone. "How far apart are the pains?" she demanded. "Damn! No, no, that's okay," she said, automatically soothing the caller. But it wasn't okay. Given her condition, Darlene should have been in the hospital on Nirvana for the blessed event, and very well might have been, if Hana had had the three more weeks she'd been counting on to convince the woman's husband it was necessary. Time and Mother Nature had made it a moot point now. "Bring her to the clinic," Hana said to the young woman's frantic husband. "We'll be ready for her."

HANA LOOKED DOWN AT the frightened young mother-to-be and smiled through her surgical mask. "How're you doing, Darlene?"

"Okay." She licked lips made dry by panting. "I think."

"Still feeling pain?"

"No."

"Good. That's real good." Hana nodded. "You just lie there and think about the beautiful baby you're going to have when this is over and we'll do the rest." She looked up at Quinn, standing on the other side of the pregnant woman, and took a deep, steadying breath. "Ready?"

He looked a little green around the gills but he smiled gamely—she could see it in the way his eyes crinkled above the mask he wore—and nodded. "Ready." *As ready as I'll ever be,* he thought.

He'd helped to deliver a baby only once before. Or, rather, been present at a birth; the woman had done all the delivering involved, telling him what to do between contractions that arched her body like a bow and had her biting back screams. It had been a routine vaginal birth, except that he and the mother-to-be were in the backseat of a parked car, with the panicked father-in-waiting hovering at the open door, silhouetted from behind by the fire that had brought on his wife's labor. He'd come away from it shaking his head, amazed at the female capacity for enduring pain, and wondering why any woman in her right mind ever had more than one child.

But that experience, harrowing as it had been, was nothing compared to what was happening in front of him now.

According to Hana's hurried explanation as she prepared herself and the examining room for a delivery, the young woman on the table between them had high blood pressure—so high that the stress of a prolonged labor could conceivably cause a stroke, or worse. The successive blood-pressure readings Hana had taken as soon as the laboring woman arrived at the clinic only confirmed her fears: each contraction drove Darlene's blood pressure higher. There was no time to get her to the hospital on Nirvana. Even if the helicopter had been right outside on the lanai, there'd have been no time. Emergency surgery was the only option.

And so, without automatic blood-pressure or fetal monitors, without any specialized equipment for premature babies, or state-of-the-art lifesaving gear in case the mother began to fail, without a properly trained assistant or even a nurse, Hana was preparing to deliver the baby by cesarean using local anesthesia. And she was doing it as coolly and calmly as if she'd performed one every day of her life. Looking at her, standing there in her drab green scrubs, her long braid pinned up and hidden under a sterile cap, the lower half of her face covered by a surgical mask, Quinn couldn't remember being prouder of anyone than he was of Hana at that very moment.

"I'm going to make a horizontal incision just

above your pubic hairline, Darlene," she said quietly, her voice deliberately pitched to soothe and pacify. "Just a small one, so you'll be able to wear your bikini when you get your figure back."

Quinn tried not to look but the barrier Hana had rigged up was only to keep Darlene from seeing the procedure; she hadn't given a thought to what effect viewing the horrors of surgically assisted childbirth would have on his delicate masculine sensibilities. He wondered again, fleetingly, why any woman would voluntarily put herself through the experience.

"I'll cut through your uterine wall next. And then..." She laid the scalpel aside. "I'll need your help now, Mike," she said, motioning him closer with a lift of her chin. "Here, hold this back. And here." She placed his fingers where she wanted them while he struggled to keep his dinner down. "That's it. Good." She took a second to glance at her patient again, her encouraging smile apparent in her eyes. "Get ready to say hello to the newest Kapaua," she said and inserted her hands into the incision she'd made.

And, suddenly, there was a baby, and Quinn abruptly ceased to wonder why women endured the rigors of pregnancy and childbirth. The squirming new life in Hana's hands was why. The infant was tinier than any human being could possibly be, smeared with blood and goo, but utterly beautiful and mewing like a kitten.

Alarmed, Quinn lifted his gaze to Hana's face.

She was smiling beautifully, staring down at the brand-new life in her hands. "It's a girl," she said. "A fine big girl. And if she's premature, I'll eat my surgical mask. I think we must have misjudged the date of conception."

"Oh, let me see," Darlene said. "Let me see her."

"Let me clean her up a bit first."

"Is she all right?"

"She's perfect," Hana reassured her. "Just perfect. Ten fingers. Ten toes. Everything right where it should be."

"Shouldn't she be screaming her head off?" Quinn whispered. Everything he knew about brand-new babies, which was admittedly very little, indicated that they came into the world with their lungs operating at top volume.

"She will be," Hana said calmly. "Here." She motioned for him to take the baby.

"Me?"

"You," Hana said, placing the tiny infant in his hands. "I need to suction her. Don't be afraid to get a good grip," she instructed, her eyes growing misty at the awkward way he was handling the baby; he held her between his big hands as if she were as fragile as a soap bubble. "She's slippery as a little fish and a lot tougher than she looks. Aren't you, sweetheart?" she said as the baby screwed up her little face. The infant sucked in a quick, startled breath, and then let it out, screaming like a miniature banshee at the indignity of what was being done to her. "That's the girl. Give us all hell."

Hana cut the cord, dropping it and the placenta into a porcelain-coated tin basin. "She's beautiful, isn't she?" she said to Quinn as she gently wiped the worst of the birth fluids from the tiny body with a warm towel. "C-section babies are lucky. They don't get all red and misshapen from the normal birth trauma."

"She looks pretty red to me."

Hana smiled and picked up a sterile receiving blanket. Draping it over one hand she took the squalling infant into her arms. "There you go now, sweetheart. The worst is over," she crooned, cradling the baby to her breast as she tucked the blanket around her tiny body. "Say hello to Mama," she said, lowering the little girl into her mother's eager arms.

While Darlene cooed and exclaimed over her new daughter, Hana moved to the open incision on her belly and quickly closed it with neat, precise sutures. A few more quick, efficient maneuvers, and the wound was covered with a sterile bandage. Only then did Hana strip off her gloves and lower her surgical mask, indicating with a nod of her head that Quinn could do the same.

"Everything looks fine," she said to the new mother. "But I'm going to send you over to the hospital on Nirvana just to make sure."

"But my husband—"

"I'll handle your husband," Hana said fiercely. "I'll tell him how lucky he was tonight—lucky he didn't lose you and that beautiful little baby you're holding."

And handle him she did, letting him know, in no uncertain terms, just what could have happened to his wife and child. Already distraught over the condition of his wife when he'd brought her in, he was trembling and remorseful when Hana got through with him—not only willing to send his wife and baby to the hospital on Nirvana, but prepared to make the trip with them.

"Whoever called women the 'weaker sex' was an idiot," Quinn said as he stood on the lanai with his arm around Hana and watched the lights of the helicopter fade into the night. He squeezed her shoulders. "You were magnificent tonight. I was shaking in my boots, but you were magnificent."

"I was shaking, too," Hana said in a tired voice. "So many things could have gone wrong."

"But they didn't."

She turned her face into his chest. "No, thank God, they didn't."

They stood like that for a few minutes longer, his arms around her shoulders, supporting her; hers wrapped around his waist, absorbing his strength. His chin rested on the top of her head. Her cheek was pressed against his chest. She could feel his heartbeat, slow and steady, and she closed her eyes and sighed, remembering him as he had been in her examining room, holding that tiny new life in his huge hands. She pictured him holding a child of theirs that way—so gently, so tenderly, with endearing awkwardness and an awestruck expression on his face—and wondered wistfully if it would ever happen for them.

In the weeks they'd been lovers, he hadn't once mentioned anything as permanent as marriage and a family. He'd said he wanted to stay. He'd said he loved her. But... Seeing his sloop still sitting at anchor in the shallow waters behind her house, looking ready to sail away on the next outgoing tide, she didn't know if he meant permanently, or only until he healed completely. And she didn't feel quite secure enough to ask.

"Hana?"

"Hmm?"

"Let's make a baby."

She drew back, startled, and peered up into his face. "Make a baby?"

"Not right this minute," he said. "You're too tired to make a baby right now. And we'll need to get married first. But let's do it soon."

Hana just stared up at him, a mild sort of shock paralyzing her tongue, a wild joy careering through her veins.

"When I saw you in there tonight, holding that baby... You looked so natural. So right. And I wondered what you'd look like with my baby in your arms." He leaned his forehead against hers. "I want you to have my baby, Hana. I want you to marry me and have my baby. What do you say?"

Her joy welled up in a single word: "Yes."

9

IT TURNED OUT THAT HANA wasn't too tired to try to make a baby. Just knowing Quinn wanted to was enough to revitalize her, sending sensual heat and energy zinging through her body, the way joy was zinging through her heart.

"Let's go swimming," she said, peering up at him in the dark.

"Swimming?" He cocked an eyebrow at her. "I'd have thought all you'd want after what you went through tonight was a hot bath and bed."

"Is that all you want?"

He smiled ruefully. "No, but I'm being considerate." His smile turned teasing. "For which I expect to be fully repaid later."

"You don't have to wait until later." She slipped out of his arms as she spoke and took a skipping half-step backward and then another, unable to contain the feelings bubbling through her blood. "Last one in's a rotten egg," she cried gleefully as she turned and dashed toward the water.

Quinn was just a half a step behind her, then was racing by her as she stumbled on the sand. "You're starting to stink already, Doc," he taunted, yanking his scrub top off over his head as he ran. He paused by the water's edge, toeing off his shoes, along with the paper booties that covered them, bouncing around on one leg as he struggled to rid himself of his scrubpants and jeans.

Hana ran by him, laughing, her bare bottom-half glinting in the moonlight, her top half lost in the folds of her faded green tunic. He grabbed for her and missed, falling to his backside on the sand just as Hana's feet hit the water. She tossed her top away from her with a triumphant shout, unaware and uncaring that it landed in the water, and turned to face him, pinching her nose with two fingers as if she'd smelled something bad.

Quinn kicked out of his pants and came up off the sand with a roar, launching himself at her in a running dive. Hana shrieked and turned to run, but the thigh-high water made the going slow. He caught her around the waist before she'd taken two steps and took her under with him. They came up sputtering and laughing, wrestling to gain the upper hand, each of them striking out toward open water only to be snatched back by a slender hand on a hairy ankle or a mammoth fist around a long black braid. They went under twice more, rolling around each other like playful otters, and then Quinn put his hands on Hana's lithe, bare waist and pulled her flush against his chest. Holding her tight, he sank below the surface of the sea and then propelled them up out of the water with the strength of his long legs.

"Show-off," Hana said, grasping at his slippery shoulders to keep her balance as they bobbed back to the sandy bottom.

"Oh, I haven't begun to show off yet." He tightened his hands around her waist, using the strength of his arms and the buoyancy of the mid-riff-high water to lift her above his head.

She gasped and straightened her arms, bracing herself for a long moment, looking down at him as he held her poised above him. Water ran off his sun-bleached blond hair in rivulets, darkening it, plastering it to his well-shaped head. Water dripped down the sharp planes of his Viking-warrior face, glinting like drops of crystal in the moonlight. Water slicked the hard muscles of his shoulders, making them smooth and slippery under her hands, and caught in the golden hairs on his upper chest, tempting her to try to capture each gleaming droplet against her tongue.

As if he'd read her mind, his own tongue snaked out and lapped at her stomach, dipping into her navel to gather the water there.

Hana sighed and unlocked her elbows, putting a hand on either side of his head, holding him lightly as he let her slide slowly down his body. His tongue blazed a trail upward, dragging along the vertical line that bisected her taut midriff, up between her breasts and the long curve of her arched throat, over her chin and, finally, to her mouth. Her legs drifted up to lock around his waist as he thrust his tongue between her lips.

Hana sighed as he broke the kiss. "How do you always know what I want?" she said against his lips.

"Because I want it, too." But he stopped her when she would have resumed the kiss, his hands tightening on her waist to keep her from moving closer to him. "Unbraid your hair," he said.

Hana unwound her arms from around his neck

and reached for the end of her braid. The wet ribbon was stubborn; she lifted it to her mouth and bit through it rather than waste precious moments trying to untie it. Then, her eyes on his face, she threaded her fingers through the thick, interwoven strands and worked them loose, so that a sheaf of heavy, wet hair spilled over her left shoulder and down her breast to float on the water between them. "Now what?"

He shifted his hands on her waist in answer, pressing against the small of her back with his fingers, pushing against her hipbones with his thumbs. She fell back obligingly, sweeping her hair back over her shoulder with a flick of her wrist, and, arching her spine, tilted her head back until it touched the water. The movement pressed her vulva against his belly with delicious friction and presented her breasts for his pleasure and heated delectation. She flexed her pelvis against him, increasing the friction, and exaggerated the arch of her back, knowing just how enticing she must look to him.

She could feel the water rolling off her shoulders and breasts and belly, see it gleaming against her skin; she could feel her hair, floating out around her head; she could feel his hot gaze, devouring her, his hands tensing on her waist, his erection pressing against her bottom.

"I wondered what you'd look like," he said. His voice was low and almost reverent. His pale eyes gleamed with the banked fires of healthy lust. "That first night in the bar when you were being such a snooty bitch and—"

"And you were acting like an arrogant jerk,"

Hana reminded him. Her caressing tone made it sound like praise.

He smiled. "And I was acting like an arrogant jerk," he conceded. "I wondered what you'd look like all wet and naked with your hair loose."

"And how do I look?"

"Like a mermaid." He lifted one hand and reached out to touch her collarbone. Fingers splayed, palm flat against her skin, he moved it—slowly, caressingly—down the length of her body, his eyes growing hotter as he watched her arch into his caress. "Like a beautiful, sexy mermaid."

Hana felt like a mermaid…a seductive ocean siren…a voluptuous sea nymph with the power to drive men mad. And herself, as well, in the process.

Her lips burned for the pressure of his. Her nipples ached, swollen with the need to be touched and tasted. Her taut belly and the long, smooth muscles of her thighs quivered with the desperate desire to feel his possession. But she hung there in his hands, her legs around his waist, floating, her body arched and aching, letting the passion build until her lover had had his fill of looking and was driven to take.

And then, finally, Quinn's hands shifted and he pulled her toward him. Slowly, so that her back remained arched and her long hair trailed in the water. "We're going to make beautiful babies," he said, sounding as if he had just made her a promise. "Beautiful babies with black hair and big brown eyes."

"Blond hair and green eyes," Hana countered.

"Yes," he agreed. "Anything you want." And

then he leaned over her, taking her breast into his mouth, adjusting her hips so he could take possession of her body.

Hana moaned as he slipped into her, all the small feminine muscles of her body convulsing around his hardness.

He groaned when he felt her helpless, heated response and slid his hands under her buttocks, pulling her hard against him.

Hana surged up out of the water then, on the screaming verge of completion, her arms reaching for him, her ankles locking tight around his waist. She raised and lowered herself against him, guided by the hard hands that cupped her buttocks, driven by desire so fierce she was near to crying with it. Her sensitized breasts rubbed against his chest as they moved; her smooth belly slipped against the hairiness of his; the supersensitive insides of her thighs and the softness of her feminine mound collided with his raging heat and hardness with increasing pressure. And still the tension mounted.

It was as if the buoyancy of the water, the lack of anything but each other to thrust against, had slowed everything down to an excruciating degree, keeping her on the edge of fulfillment but not letting her cross over.

"I can't stand it," she sobbed, her arms tight around his neck as they strove for completion. "Not... Not another second. I can't."

"Yes, you can," Quinn breathed into her neck. "Oh, yes, you—" he reached between them and touched the hard little nubbin between her legs, rubbing it lightly with his thumb "—can."

Hana stiffened in glorious, gut-wrenching release and cried out his name. Quinn groaned in satisfaction and wrapped his arms around her, letting his own release take him.

"And that," he said, a long moment later, "is showing off."

"HE'S JUST GOT AN OLD, garden-variety cold," Hana told the mother of the cranky two-year-old who was glaring at her from the top of the examining table in her new Ivory Blush examining room. "You can give him any of the over-the-counter infant medications for the sniffling and sneezing if you follow the directions exactly. But no aspirin," she warned, holding the earpieces of her stethoscope to the little boy's ears so he could listen to her heart while she talked to his mother. "Give him plenty of fluids—water or fruit juice, preferably. And make sure he gets plenty of rest."

The mother rolled her eyes at the last piece of advice.

Hana laughed. "Well, just try to make sure he plays quietly, then. He'll be fine," she said, ruffling the child's hair. "Won't you, Kenny?"

"Tick-tock." He put his hand on her chest and patted it. "Tick-tock."

"Tick-tock," Hana agreed, smiling as the child's mother gathered up her son, a stuffed porpoise and a ratty old "blankie" she said he still refused to go anywhere without.

She stood in the examining room for a moment after they'd left, her hand on her belly, wondering if she and Quinn had made a baby the other night when they'd made love in the water. Or, she thought, smiling, if the miracle of conception had happened any of the nine or ten times they'd made love since then.

It could have happened their very first night together, of course—things had been so incendiary and had happened so fast that neither of them had thought to use anything to prevent it—but she knew for an indisputable fact that it hadn't. And they'd used birth control since then, right up until the night when the Mighty Quinn had asked her to marry him and have his baby.

She still couldn't believe it. But the wedding was planned for two weeks hence and, with any luck at all, she'd be a pregnant bride. Her periods had always been fairly regular, and by her calculations she was a day late. A day or two more, and she'd put it to the test.

"Doc Hana?" Kim stuck her head in the door, smiling when she saw the dreamy look on her employer's face. "Caught you daydreaming again," she accused with a smile. "Planning your wedding dress?"

Hana grinned and shook her head. "Planning the nursery," she said.

Kim's eyebrows rose. "You pregnant already?"

"No," Hana hastened to assure her. "Not yet. Well, at least, I'm not sure. But I hope so."

"Well, with that stud muffin you've got keeping you warm at night, you probably are."

Hana's smile widened. *Stud muffin.* She'd have to remember to tell Mike that one; he'd get a real kick out of being called a stud muffin. "Is my next patient here yet?"

"That's what I came in to tell you. Patsy Kwano

is here with her two kids. They look like they have the same thing Kenny Peterson does. All the little ones on the island seem to be passing it a—" The telephone rang, interrupting her. "I'll get that and send Patsy and the kids in," she said, and disappeared.

Hana sat down at the little desk in the corner of the examining room to make a quick note in Kenny Peterson's file before Kim ushered her next patients into the room. She glanced up a moment later, a smile of professional concern and welcome on her face as the door opened again. Her smile faded at the look on her receptionist's face. "Kim. What is it? What's the matter?"

"There's been an accident at the hotel site."

"Mike?" Hana said, fear clutching at her heart. "Is Mike hurt?"

"I don't know. The caller was kind of rushed. He just said part of the building had collapsed and they needed a doctor. And then he hung up."

Hana's face went deathly pale. *Collapsed. The building had collapsed.* Mike's worst nightmare had happened again. *Please, God,* she prayed, *don't let him have been inside this time.*

THE FIRE TRUCK MIKE had found for them was already at the site, sitting in front of the collapsed portion of the building, but there was no one in or around it as far as she could see. She could see Bennie Chu, and Big Louie, and a couple of the other volunteers digging through the rubble. But she didn't see Mike.

"You can't go over there," someone said, grabbing Hana's arm as she headed toward the truck.

"I'm looking for Mike Quinn," she said, trying to shake him off.

"Don't know him," the man said. "But you still can't go over there. It's too dangerous."

"Why is the truck sitting off to the side? Why aren't they fighting the fire?"

"Because there isn't a fire. Not yet, anyway. And there probably won't be. None of the wiring was in that section yet."

"But the smoke…?"

"Isn't smoke. It's dust. Yeah, all right. I'm coming," he hollered at someone who'd hollered at him. "You stay away from there," he said to Hana before he hurried away.

She grabbed another man by the arm as he passed her. "Mike Quinn? Have you seen him?"

"Nope." He started to shake her off, then paused, eyeing her lab coat and the medical bag in her left hand. "You the doctor?"

"Yes. Yes, I'm the doctor. But I'm looking for Mike Quinn. Has anyone seen him?"

"Well, thank God you're here," the man said, ignoring her question. "We got a lotta men need medical attention." He wrapped a beefy hand around her upper arm. "Right over here."

Hana had no choice but to go with him, but she dragged her heels, looking back over her shoulder at the pile of rubble behind her. *Is Mike trapped inside there? Trapped and maybe injured? Fighting panic? Oh, Mike!* she thought. *No man should have to live through that nightmare twice.*

"We got a spot set up for you here," the man holding her arm said. It was set off from the area of main destruction, out of the way of men who were digging through the rubble, and was cordoned off by a rough fence of sawhorses and two-by-fours. Two men were erecting a crude lean-to out of canvas and scraps of lumber to protect the injured from the sun. Half a football field away the emergency helicopter was lifting off the smooth asphalt of the future hotel parking lot, a stretcher attached to the pods on either side, headed for the hospital on Nirvana.

On the return trip, Hana knew, it would be bringing back additional medical supplies and personnel to help deal with the crisis. But right now, she was the only doctor on Paradise, and she was needed. She closed her mind to the thought of Mike trapped under the collapsed pile of rubble because there was nothing in the whole wide world she could do about it if he was, and went to work.

"Bobby Kapaua." She bent over Paradise's newest daddy where he sat braced against a sawhorse. There was blood running down the side of his face and he held his right arm cradled against his waist. "How are you doing?"

"I'm okay, Doc. I think it's just a broken collarbone, is all. There are others who need you worse."

"Let's just check this bleeding," she said, brushing back his hair to get at the source. "Superficial," she pronounced, then, softly, afraid of what his answer would be, she asked, "Did you see Mike in there?"

"No. Sorry, Doc. We were working in different sections of the hotel."

She nodded, her head bent as she dug into her

medical bag, trying furiously to keep the tears and panic at bay. "Here, hold this pad against your head. The bleeding will stop in a few minutes." She straightened and went on to the next man.

"He can wait," she said, when she'd examined him. She raised her voice. "Anyone with a simple fracture can wait. I want to look at excessive bleeding or anyone having trouble breathing or who's unconscious, first. If you're breathing and you're ambulatory, you can wait."

"Over here, Doc," someone called, and Hana went to bend over a man who'd been pulled out from under a steel beam. There was no blood but his breathing was so labored and raspy that Hana knew it was only a matter of time if something wasn't done quickly. But there was nothing she could do. "Internal injuries," she said to the men who'd appointed themselves her helpers. "Possible punctured lung. He's the next one on the helicopter to Nirvana."

She moved on to cut a blood-soaked pant leg away from a man's thigh, not even bothering to draw back as the blood spurted out over her lab coat. "His femoral artery's been cut." She pressed her hand over the wound. "I need a pressure bandage. That's it, there." She grabbed it out of the hand that offered it, folded it over with a flip of her wrist and placed it over the wound, pressing hard. "Give me your shirt," she said to another man.

He stripped it off without a word of protest.

"Okay, wrap it around his leg, over the bandage. Not too tight." She slipped her hand out from under the shirt. "Knot it right over the wound. That's it. A little tighter," she instructed.

"It has to be tight enough to stop the bleeding but not tight enough to cut off the circulation. Okay, good. Who's next?"

And so it went for the next hour. Hana bandaged and soothed, mended and ministered to those injured and in shock, fighting to keep the knowledge that she hadn't yet seen Mike from clawing its way to the forefront of her mind. She focused on each man before her, assessing his injuries, doing what she could, and then moving on to the next.

After a while she'd begun to realize things weren't as bad as they'd seemed at first. Aside from four cases serious enough to require hospitalization, including the two who'd been airlifted before she arrived, and one case of severe shock, all the rest were cuts and bruises and broken bones. And even then, there weren't as many of those as she'd first thought.

"It was the smallest of the three buildings," said a man whose head she was stitching. "Something in one of the corners collapsed and just dragged the whole thing over with it. It looks like it's kinda leanin' over to its side."

"Must have been that shipment of supplies came in last week," said someone else. "I told the foreman those crossbeams didn't look regulation."

With the last two serious cases ready to be whisked off to the hospital on Nirvana, and the remaining wounded so few and so superficial that the doctor who'd been flown over to help had decided to go back with them, Hana's mind was free to focus on her one real fear.

It threatened to overwhelm her. *Mike must be inside the collapsed building,* she thought. There was no other place he could be. He hadn't been among the wounded. No one she'd talked to remembered seeing him after that section had collapsed. And if he was able, wouldn't he have come to find her at the first opportunity? Or at least sent a message, if he couldn't be spared from his duties? Wouldn't he have known she'd be worried and sick with fear?

She started walking toward the men working on the small mountain of rubble that had once been a three-story building. Ignoring everything but her own need to know where Quinn was, she stepped around the sawhorse barriers meant to keep all but the rescue workers out of the danger area. If Mike wasn't with her, then he was somewhere in that hell of twisted steel and concrete. And nothing on earth would keep her from getting as close to him as she could.

"Louie," she called, seeing a familiar face among the off-islanders who made up the bulk of the construction crew. "Big Louie!"

"Doc Hana." He looked down at the blood splashed across her lab coat and the khaki shorts and white blouse beneath. "You all right?"

"It's not my blood." She waved his concern away, her mind on vitally more important matters. "Have you seen Mike?"

Big Louie looked away.

"Oh, God! He's dead, isn't he?" She clutched at the front of the big man's shirt, frantic with sudden, overwhelming fear. "He was trapped in the building and he's dead!"

"No, Doc. No." Big Louie covered her hands with his. "He isn't dead."

"Not dead?"

"He isn't even hurt."

"He's not hurt? Then— Then *where is he?*" She screamed the words in his face.

"Right over there on the other side of the fire truck," Big Louie said, pointing. "Sittin' on the—"

But Hana had already cast him aside from her and was running frantically in the direction he'd pointed. "Mike? Mike? Where are you?" She rounded the front fender of the big truck, nearly falling in her haste to scramble around it. "Mike, are you—" She came to a dead stop. "Mike?" she said softly.

He lifted his head from his hands at the sound of her voice and looked up at her with bleak, hollow, empty eyes.

"Oh, Mike. What is it?" She took a step forward, hands outstretched, reaching out to hold and comfort him. Big Louie had said he wasn't hurt—and there wasn't a mark or a scratch on him—but he looked...*maimed* was the only word that came to mind. He was sitting there on the running board of the old fire truck he was so proud of, his big body slumped in an attitude of utter defeat. He was as white as a sheet beneath his tan, and there were beads of sweat on his forehead and temples. But his skin, when she touched him, was icy cold. "Where are you hurt?"

He flinched away from her.

"Mike? What is it? Please, sweetheart—" She put her hands on his face and turned it up to hers. "Tell me what's the matter so I can help you."

He didn't jerk his head away but he refused to look at her. "Nothing can help me," he said. His voice was flat and without inflection.

"*I'll* help you," she said fiercely. "Just tell me what it is and *I'll* help you."

"You can't. Nothing can."

"But—"

He lifted his eyes to hers again—those desolate, lifeless eyes. They chilled Hana to the bone, causing tears of fear and dread to cloud her sight. What could possibly be so wrong that he would look at her like that?

"I'm afraid," he said. "There's a man trapped in there and I can't help him because I'm afraid!"

10

WITHOUT A WORD, HANA drew Mike's head to her breast and held him, simply held him, trying to infuse all of her warmth and love into him.

"It's all right, Mike," she said softly, choking back her tears as she stroked his sweat-dampened hair. He held himself stiffly, refusing to return or even accept her embrace. It scared her. The remoteness and detached docility, the utter stillness, wasn't like him. The Mighty Quinn she knew and loved was larger than life, full of bravado and ego and endless roguish charm.

Shock? she wondered, knowing the kind brought on by emotional upheaval was often infinitely more devastating than that induced by a physical cause. And witnessing a re-creation of an event that had caused so much pain—physical, emotional and spiritual—had to be more devastating than anyone could really know unless they'd suffered through it.

"It's all right," she said again, not knowing what else to do, what else to say. "Everybody is afraid sometime. Of something. And you've earned your fear."

"I should be in there," Quinn said dully. "It's my job. It's what I was trained for. I should be in there."

"No," Hana said. "No, you *shouldn't* be in there. Not after what you've been through. No one expects it of you."

"I expect it of me."

"Then you're wrong," she said. When he didn't respond, she grasped his hair and pulled his head back. "Do you hear me, Michael Quinn? You're wrong. You're not Superman." Her words were fierce and passionate as she stared down into his empty green eyes. "You're not some mighty mythical Viking god, no matter what you think or what anyone calls you. You're a human being and you've had a terrible, life-altering experience. Anyone with an ounce of compassion understands that and doesn't expect you to—"

"An ounce of *pity*, you mean," he said, and his eyes narrowed with the first flash of emotion she'd seen since he'd lifted his head from his hands.

"All right, have it your way," she said, realizing she'd been trying to reach him in exactly the wrong way. The Mighty Mike Quinn wasn't a man to be brought around by soft words and sympathy. Well, then, fine! She'd make him angry enough to want to reach out and choke her if that's what it took. She pushed his head away from her with a deliberately disdainful gesture and stepped back. "Call it pity if it will make you feel better. Lord knows, you're wallowing in it. Oceans and oceans of self-pity!"

He recoiled as if she'd struck him, looking up at her as if she'd betrayed him.

Hana wavered but pushed on, instinctively knowing it was the right way, the only way, to pull him back from wherever he'd gone. "Only a man obsessed with the image of himself as some kind of fallen hero would just sit there, drowning his sorrows in an orgy of self-pity, while another man dies.''

"I can't go in there!" He rose to his feet and advanced on her, grabbing her by the upper arms. His eyes blazed with fury and pain. "Don't you understand?" he demanded, shaking her. *"I can't go in there!"*

"I know you can't go in there," Hana shouted back. "And I wouldn't want you to even if you could. But there are other things you can do. Other ways you can help." She forced herself to lower her voice and speak more calmly, though no less intensely. "You're the only man here with any heavy-rescue experience. The rest of them are willing but they don't know what to do or how to do it. You do. You could tell them. Direct them."

"But I'm afraid," he said in a low voice, as if it were an added shame just to say the words out loud. "And they know it."

"So? They're afraid, too. We're all afraid."

He looked stunned for a moment, as if what she'd just said were a novel concept, something he'd never even considered. And, in truth, it was. Oh, he'd heard it before, but he didn't really believe it—not at a gut level, not down inside himself where he lived; because before he'd been trapped in that building, before he'd lost his faith in himself, he'd never been afraid. Not ever. And he'd assumed that the men who did the same job he did weren't afraid, either, despite what other people might say. Or else, how could they have done their jobs? How could they have forced themselves into dangerous, life-threatening situations time after time if they were feeling even a tenth of the fear he was feeling now? That they might have done just that, altered his whole concept of…everything.

"They're all afraid," Hana said again, tilting her head toward the men trying to move the rubble of the collapsed building off their fallen comrade. "But that hasn't stopped them from doing what has to be done." She pinned him with an accusing stare, trying to inject some scorn into her expression, when all she really wanted to do was take him in her arms and soothe his fears away. "Are you going to let it stop you?"

He stared at her for a long moment, fear and hope, anger and nascent joy warring for prominence in his eyes. And then he made a deep noise, something between an anguished sob and a triumphant shout, and pulled her into his arms. It was suddenly all so clear to him. Everything. His fear. His life. Even the damned difference between sympathy and pity. Everything. Somehow, with her words, with her love, with the sheer force of her personality, Hana had dragged him out of hiding and back into the real world. He was still shaking and sweating, still afraid; but he knew, now, that he could do what had to be done. He *would* do it, dammit, because she believed he could. And he *could*.

"Damn you, Hana," he said, crushing her to him. "Damn you."

It's going to be all right, Hana thought, sagging against him. "I love you," she said, her voice muffled against his muscled chest. Her arms were as hard around him as his were around her. The tears flowing unheeded down her cheeks were the tears of a woman welcoming her man back from the wars. *Thank God, it's going to be all right!*

They stood locked tight in the safety and security of each other's arms, absorbing each other's strength and love, loath to let each other go. But they both knew they must.

"You'd better go," Hana said, bravely pulling out of Quinn's embrace. Bravely, because she didn't want to let him go at all. Not now. Not ever. "They need you more than I do right now."

"I'm going to love you till the day I die," Quinn said, and kissed her. Hard.

And then he was stepping away, reaching for the hard hat he'd dropped on the running board a mere lifetime ago. "Stay close," he said, as he settled it on his head. "We'll need you when we bring him out."

Hana smiled up at him through the glimmer of tears in her eyes, daring to tease him, just a little, now that she had him back. He wasn't whole yet—he might never be completely whole—but he was back, the Mighty Mike Quinn in all his glory. "Try to remember that you don't always have to be the hero."

He nodded and touched his index finger to the brim of his hat in a brief salute. And then he was gone, striding around the front of the truck, calling to his volunteer fire-fighting force.

Hana hurried after him, needing to keep him in sight, even if she couldn't do anything to help yet. She followed as far as the sawhorse barrier, grasping it tightly in both hands as he stepped around it and approached the men.

"Get those men off that pile of rubble," he said with a new note of confidence and authority in his voice. "And get everybody out of the way who doesn't need to be here. This isn't a damned carnival. And I want absolute quiet. Starting now."

Such was the force of his personality that most of the men automatically moved to do his bidding, glad to have someone take charge who might actually know what he was doing. Only one man balked, raising his arm to stay the others. "And who put you in charge?" he challenged.

"I did," Quinn said, standing his ground as the man stalked over to stare him right in the eye. "I'm the only one here with any heavy-rescue experience."

"Then, why the hell have you been sitting over there—" the man jerked his head toward the fire truck "—with your head in your hands?"

"Because I let fear get the better of me for a while," Quinn said honestly, unflinchingly, his body braced for whatever derision the other man—or any of the other men—might heap on him for that admission. When they only stood there looking at him, he went on. "But then I had it pointed out to me that everyone else is afraid, too, and that fear is no reason not to do your job."

"How do we know you won't go catatonic on us again?"

"You don't," Quinn said. "But, then, I don't know that you won't fall apart at some point, either."

The man seemed to swell at the insult implicit in

the words, and his fists clenched around the handle of the shovel he was holding.

"Save it," Quinn said, refusing to let himself be drawn into a fight. "You're going to need your strength."

He looked away from the man then, past his shoulder, and scanned the faces ringed around them. Bennie Chu stared back at him. And Big Louie. And Peterson. And the rest of the men who'd volunteered to safeguard the citizens of Paradise. Their faces were dirt-streaked and haggard, and in their expressions he saw an understandable wariness mixed with a willingness to follow and, almost to a man, the hope that he could provide the direction they so desperately needed. He prayed to God he wouldn't let them down again.

"We'll tunnel in from the side, shoring up as we go," he said. "We'll need some short timbers for that. Peterson, you see about those...."

They worked ceaselessly for the next few hours—two or three or, perhaps, more. Hana lost all track of time as she stood at the barrier watching, her nerves screaming, winding tighter and tighter as time slipped by in slow motion.

The other onlookers—the wives and girlfriends and children, the townspeople—stood in utter silence behind the barriers, just as Hana stood, watching and waiting and praying. They seemed to know, almost instinctively, of the need to be silent, of how the slightest noise at the wrong pitch could set things to shifting and crumbling. There was no noise, and hardly any movement at all, as if the entire population of Paradise was holding its collective breath until the crisis was over. Even the rescue helicopter was silent, its blades still as the pilot waited in the hope of airlifting a patient to Nirvana.

Load after careful load of concrete and rubble was scooped up and carted away in wheelbarrows and by hand. Steel beams were lifted, as delicately and carefully as if they were straws in a game of pick-up-sticks. It was painstaking, nerve-racking, exacting work and it had to be done at breakneck speed because a man's life depended on it.

A few of the rescue workers dropped from fatigue or heat exhaustion or the sudden onset of delayed shock. Another few more were injured in small cave-ins as hunks of broken concrete or pieces of pipe were pulled out too soon or not soon enough and sections of rubble tumbled unexpectedly. For some small stretch of time, Hana would have something blessedly constructive to do for however long it took to tend to the wounded. But then she was back at the barrier, like everyone else, watching. Except that she watched one man only—acutely, painfully aware of the effect each such mishap had on him.

She could see the unnatural tenseness in his shoulders, see the strain and apprehension in his eyes each time she looked at him, even if no one else could. She could see the way his jaw clenched every time the debris shifted or settled. But he didn't falter. He was afraid, yes, but he was facing his fear and not letting it turn him away from what had to be done.

That was the real definition of courage, Hana thought as she applied a gauze dressing to a minor abrasion. She doubted she could ever convince the Mighty Quinn of it, of course, but she would try. Later, when they were alone in the dark, safe and secure in each other's arms, she would tell him how proud he had made her.

"It isn't brave to do a thing that holds no terrors for you," she would say, "even if it looks like bravery to other people. What's brave is to face the thing that has you shaking in your shoes and do it anyway."

As he was doing now.

He didn't crawl into the tunnel they were digging—she didn't blame him for that, and was, in fact, grateful he hadn't conquered his fear to that extent—but he was everywhere else. He added his strength to Big Louie's, straining to lever a huge slab of concrete out of the way. He hauled away debris that had been brought to the mouth of the tunnel by the relays of men who'd been able to swallow their fear and crawl inside. He shored up faltering determination and gave the weary men a tireless example to follow.

Her heart in her throat, Hana watched him crouch down by the opening to the tunnel, his head bent as he spoke to the man just emerging. Something in his expression alerted her to the fact that there was a problem.

They were speaking too softly for her to hear what was said from where she was, but she could see Quinn's lips move. "Are you sure?" she saw him say, and then, "Goddammit. Goddamit all to hell!"

He stood, his head swinging around, his gaze coming to rest on Hana. She straightened away from the barrier and stood, tense and fearful, as he came toward her.

"They got to him but his foot's caught under a section of the roof that's too damned big to move," Quinn said without preamble. "We're going to have to take his foot off to get him out of there."

Hana paled. "Oh, my God. Are you sure?"

"It's his foot or his life, Hana. There's no other way."

"Yes, of course," she said, visibly gathering herself together. "I've got painkillers and antiseptics in my bag but I'll have to send someone back to the clinic for a bone saw."

"Do it fast," Quinn said and turned back to the evacuation site.

The fifteen-minute wait for her bone saw seemed like fifteen hours. But it arrived, finally, and Hana had no choice but to do what must be done. Taking it and her bag, she ducked under the barrier and made her way toward the mouth of the tunnel.

"I'm ready," she said, announcing herself.

Quinn looked up. "What the hell are you doing on this side of the barrier? Get back over there where you belong."

"I brought the bone saw." She held it up.

Quinn grabbed it out of her hand. "Fine. Now get back over there."

"I've got the painkillers and antiseptic, too. And some sterile pressure bandages." She smiled, too brightly, trying to show him it wasn't going to be all that bad. "I'm ready."

"Ready for what?"

Hana motioned toward the mouth of the tunnel. "To go in there."

"Like hell you are!" The words were spoken in a furious whisper that somehow managed to sound like a roar. He took her arm and turned her around, ready to march her back to safety. "You shouldn't even be this close, dammit."

Hana balked. "I'm the only doctor here. I have to go in."

"No."

"Mike, the man needs medical attention."

"I said no."

"But Mike—"

"No, Hana. You're not going in there and that's final. Somebody else can do it."

"Somebody else isn't a doctor. I am."

"You're still not going in."

"And what if he dies?"

"Then he dies," Quinn said. "But I'm not risking you."

"I'm not yours to risk, dammit."

"The hell you aren't!" They were standing nose to nose now, shouting at each other in furious whispers, ever mindful of the need for quiet. "You're my woman and in two weeks you'll be my wife." His gaze dropped to her stomach. "You may even be the mother of my child. Have you thought of that?"

"We can't risk a man's life on a maybe, Mike."

"When it concerns you and our unborn child, I can."

"Then who's going to go in and do it? You?"

He flinched at that but stood his ground. "I would if it were the only way to keep you out," he said, hoping to God it was true. "But this calls for a steady hand. And I haven't got that anymore— not in a situation like this. Bennie's going to do it. He's already been in and assessed the situation."

"Bennie? Bennie's not a doctor."

"But I've helped you plenty of times, Hana," Bennie said as he came up to them. He reached out and took the bone saw from Quinn. "I can handle it."

Hana yanked her arm out of Quinn's hand and whirled to face Bennie. "An amputation, Bennie? Can you handle an amputation? Do you know how much painkiller to give, and where? Or are you just planning to cut off his foot without any and listen to him scream? Do you know what to do for the bleeding? Can you—"

"That's enough, Hana," Quinn said, cutting across her impassioned tirade. He reached for her medical bag. "Let go," he said, wresting it from her when she refused to release it. He handed it to Bennie and then grabbed her by both arms and shoved her back, straight into Big Louie's arms. "Take her back to the barrier," he ordered the other man. "And make sure she stays there."

Then he turned and walked back toward the tunnel.

"Mike? Dammit, Mike, you can't do this!" But he had, and Hana had no choice but to go with Big Louie.

She stood at the barrier with her overgrown watchdog, watching as her medical bag and the saw were passed to the men in the tunnel to be handed down the line until they reached the man trapped inside, watching as Quinn and Bennie stood off to one side, quietly conferring about the next step.

Hana knew that the amputation would be a makeshift operation, even if she were doing it herself. Under the circumstances, it couldn't be anything else. But at least she could make it less traumatic for the wounded man. She could make sure as little damage as possible was done to his bones and tissue, so that the operation wouldn't have to be done over again, causing him to lose even more of his leg.

And, dammit, it was her job! It was what she had been born to do. Trained to do. And no man with big muscles and a warrior complex was going to stop her from doing it!

Taking advantage of Big Louie's preoccupation with what was going on by the mouth of the tunnel, Hana ducked underneath the barrier and sprinted across the rubble-filled site. She was over halfway to her goal before he realized she'd escaped him.

"Doc Hana!" he hollered, forgetting to keep his voice down as he went charging after her. "Doc Hana—Ah!" He fell heavily as a piece of masonry shifted beneath his massive form.

His shout brought Quinn's head up. "Dammit, keep your voice— *Hana!*" The word was an anguished whisper of sound. And then he was racing toward her, trying to reach her before she ducked inside the tunnel.

He was too late.

She was already beyond his reach, half crawling, scrambling awkwardly over the men inside who'd served as a relay team for her medical bag and saw. They did the same for her, pushing and shoving her over their supine bodies toward the injured man at the tunnel's end in the mistaken belief that that's what had been intended all along.

"Dammit, stop her," Quinn hissed at the first man in the tunnel.

The man tried to obey but it was useless. Hana had already scrambled over him and the next two men in line, intent on reaching her objective. Quinn dropped to his hands and knees and started in after her. "Hana!" he bellowed, forgetting the need for silence.

Someone jerked him back with a hand at the collar of his shirt just as a shower of grit shifted down through the ceiling of the tunnel.

"There're too many in there already," Bennie said when Quinn tried to shake him off. "And she'll fight you. Man, think!" He tightened his grip on Quinn's shirt as Quinn continued to move forward into the tunnel. "You go crawling in there after her and try to drag her out over all those men, you'll bring the whole thing down around your ears."

Quinn went as still as death, fighting every instinct he possessed that was urging him to go in after her, to rush to the rescue of his woman, whether she wanted to be rescued or not. But he knew Bennie was right. He'd been in an eerily similar situation before, after the Mexico City earthquake of 1985. He and his crew had tunneled through to a woman who was literally pinned like a butterfly on a specimen board, held down by the jagged end of a splintered timber skewered through her side. They'd formed a human conveyor belt then, too, prepared to pass her unconscious body hand-over-hand once they'd finally cut her free.

And then a small dog had somehow edged its way into the tunnel—the woman's dog, as it turned out—barking frantically as it scented its mistress. Someone had grabbed it, muffling it before any real damage could result, but the shrill barks had been enough to bring grit and small rocks tumbling down from the unstable ceiling of the tunnel, causing everyone to freeze until the danger of a cave-in was judged to have passed.

The same thing could happen now, with Hana inside. If he went in after her and she struggled... If there was any noise... God, he could have brought the tunnel in on her with his mindless caterwauling! He swallowed, forcing down all his natural instincts, and backed out of the tunnel entrance. He stood, turning to look at Bennie, and found himself facing nearly every man on the site who wasn't in the tunnel.

They stared at him, silently asking what he intended to do. The man trapped under the pile of rubble was an off-islander and, while they sincerely wanted to bring him to safety, none of them had a personal stake in his survival. But Hana Jamieson was an important person on Paradise, well liked and well respected, aside from her value as the island's only doctor.

"If you can't do it," one of the men said into the silence, "I'll go in after her."

Quinn didn't even notice the implied slur on his manhood. "No," he said, his fear of being trapped overridden by his fear for Hana. "She's my woman. I'll bring her out."

11

A SHOWER OF PEBBLES FELL from the ceiling, pelting her back a split second after Quinn shouted her name. Hana froze, paralyzed with uncertainty and fear, until someone planted a hand on her rump and pushed her off him. She scrambled forward again without realizing that the man beneath her had pushed against her in an effort to propel himself in the opposite direction.

Blood was pounding in her fingertips and at her temples, as loudly as a snare drum in the silence that surrounded her. She heard a man coughing in the choking dust, and it sounded like thunder rumbling overhead. She tensed, waiting for another pelting of rocks and dust. None fell.

Keep calm, Hana told herself, fighting down panic as she forced herself to start crawling again. *Be calm. Stay calm. It was only a little dust. The tunnel's not falling in. Stay calm.* She repeated it silently, like a litany, knowing it was the only way she was going to be able to keep going. Each inch, each foot of progress into the mountain of rubble, required more and more effort. She could feel the sides of the tunnel pressing down on her, closing in by minute fractions of inches so that she wanted to scramble backward to freedom, and to hell with doing what was right and noble.

How had Mike stood it? How did the men she was crawling over now, stand it? How could they lie there, unmoving, when the tunnel rumbled and groaned as if it were alive? What kept them from bolting for the safety of light and air? And then she realized they weren't lying immobile, that they *were* bolting. Slowly and carefully, perhaps, but they were leaving, squirming out from under her as she crawled over them.

Hana bit back a whimper and kept going, trying not to dwell on her fear. But she was so scared. So damned scared. More scared than she had ever been in her life. And if she was this scared, having never experienced a cave-in, how much worse must it be for someone who had been trapped in one?

It was no wonder Mike had nightmares about the last one he'd been in, she thought, trying desperately to keep her mind off her own fear. And it was truly amazing that he'd managed to pull himself together enough to help with this one. She wouldn't have blamed him a bit if he'd run and hid. It was what she felt like doing.

But she didn't.

Calm, she told herself, and kept crawling toward the feeble yellow light ahead of her, praying that she wouldn't collapse into a whimpering heap of abject terror and have to be rescued herself.

Her goal, when she finally reached it, was hardly bigger than the tunnel she'd crawled through, and only about a half a foot higher. The rescue workers had managed to dig out a small circular space around the trapped man, clearing away all the rubble except for what was holding him down. A small battery-powered lantern supplied the faint golden light that had guided her.

Her patient lay as still as death, his face covered with streaks of dirt and sweat, his eyes wide open and pleading as he watched her emerge from the darkness. Responding to the silent plea, Hana pushed herself upright and came the rest of the way on her knees.

"It's all right," she whispered, reaching out to touch him when she got close enough. He grasped her hand and held on so tightly that she thought her bones might break. "I'm a doctor." She leaned over him, brushing at the dirt and grit with her free hand. "You're going to be all right."

"My foot?" His voice was thin with panic and pain.

Hana bit her lip, wondering whether it would be best to lie. "I'll have to look at it before I can tell you anything," she said, hoping it wasn't as bad as Quinn had said, but knowing it was.

Even without a close inspection, it looked as if a portion of what once had been the ceiling had come down on his ankle, pinning it to what had been the floor. She was surprised that his foot hadn't been completely severed, so severe was the compression.

"Let me give you something for the pain," Hana said. "And then I'll have a look at your foot." She tugged at her hand.

"You won't leave me?" he pleaded.

"No," Hana said, thinking of another man who'd pleaded with her not to leave him. She hadn't been around for that man when it really mattered, but she'd do what she could for this one. "No, I won't leave you. I promise."

He nodded, reassured by the look in her eyes, and let go of her hand.

Hana squirmed around and snagged her medical bag. "What's your name?" she asked as she pulled it toward her.

"Ross. Ross Beecham."

"Do you have a family?"

"I have a daughter. Kelly. She lives with her mother."

Hana lifted the hypodermic, squinting at it in the dim light. "How old is your little girl?"

"Seven. No, seven and a half," he corrected himself, trying for a smile. "She always reminds me of the half."

"I'll bet she's a real charmer," Hana said as she swabbed his skin with alcohol.

"I'll show you a picture when we get out of here."

"You do that." Hana administered the shot. "There, that should do it. A few minutes and you won't feel a thing."

"Actually, I don't feel much of anything right now except a kind of throbbing."

"That's the body's automatic defense system," Hana said. "When you've suffered a severe trauma, it kind of shuts the pain sensors off for a while. Believe me—" she patted his shoulder "— you'll feel it later. Now, let's have a look at that foot."

She picked up the lantern as she spoke, shuffling sideways on her knees to get nearer his trapped foot, bending over for a closer look. It was all she could do not to gasp in horror. There didn't look to be even an inch of space between the two sections of concrete that held him prisoner. The leg above his ankle was already swelling, pushing at the heavy fabric of his pants like too much air against the skin of a balloon. Gangrene would soon be a factor if it wasn't already.

"How bad is it, Doc?"

Hana couldn't lie to him. "Bad," she said. "There's no way to get it free." She turned and looked into his eyes, reaching out to take his hand, trying to soften the blow as she delivered her prognosis. "I'm going to have to amputate your foot."

To her surprise, he only nodded. "Do it fast."

"Yes." Hana squeezed his fingers and withdrew her hand from his. She was digging through her medical bag for her instruments when another shower of grit and small rocks pelted them.

"Do it real fast," he said and closed his eyes.

Hana took a deep breath and willed her hands to stop trembling. She was a doctor and she had a patient who needed her. That was all that mattered right now. It was all she should be thinking about. Her hands stopped shaking. Taking a deep breath, she picked up her scissors and began cutting away the fabric of Ross Beechem's pant leg.

"Hana?" A soft voice came out of the darkness of the tunnel. "Hana, are you all right?"

She looked toward the sound. "Mike?"

"Thank God you're all right," he said, pulling himself into the glow of the lantern.

"Oh, my God, Mike! What are you doing in

here?'' She glanced at the ceiling. "Get out of here before something happens."

"Not without you."

"I can't leave yet." She looked down at the man lying between them. "I promised."

He nodded and scooted closer. "Put this on," he said, handing her a hard hat. "And then tell me what to do."

"I've already given him an anesthetic," she said, not wasting any time in useless arguments; she knew that look on the Mighty Quinn's dirt-streaked face well enough to know he wasn't crawling back down that tunnel without her, no matter what demons were clawing at him. She put the hard hat on. "I wasn't going to give him anything to knock him out because I thought I might need him awake to help me get him out of here. But you're here now, so I—"

"No," Ross Beecham said clearly, though his eyes were still closed. "I want to know what's happening."

Hana didn't waste any time arguing with him, either. "All right." She looked up at Quinn. "Let's get started. You finish cutting his pant leg—" she slapped the scissors into his palm and reached into her bag for a bottle of alcohol "—while I sterilize my instruments."

Quinn edged nearer, his gaze scanning the injured man's leg and the two slabs of concrete that held him prisoner. "Wait."

"We can't wait," Hana said, but she leaned over inquiringly, trying to see what Quinn was looking at so intently.

He'd had to take his crew's word for it that the

man's foot was going to have to be amputated, but now that he'd had a chance to look over the situation himself, he wasn't so sure. He stuck the pointed end of the scissors he held in the crack between the floor and ceiling. It wasn't much, but maybe... "I think I can get his foot loose."

"How?"

"I need something I can use as a crowbar. Something short and strong." He turned, scanning the small area for something he could use as a tool. "And relatively narrow so I can— Here. This might do it."

He closed his hand over a length of pipe embedded in the shored-up tunnel wall and, very gently, testing the resistance, pulled. A fine layer of dust and grit sifted down from the ceiling. Hana bent over her patient to keep it from coating his face. Quinn pulled a fraction of an inch more. A middling-to-large chunk of concrete rolled from the wall and clattered to the floor.

"I don't want to die," Hana said softly.

"Neither do I," Quinn said. "And we're not going to." He reached across the supine body of their patient and took her hand. "Not until we're old and gray and surrounded by our great-grandchildren," he said, staring into her eyes, willing her to believe him, willing her to trust him to take care of her.

Hana gazed back at him for a long, charged moment, trying to decipher all she saw in his eyes. There was fear there, yes, but it was under control, with no hint of the panic she'd seen earlier. And there was strength, too, and surety and self-confidence and the fierce courage of a man dead-set on doing his job no matter what the risk to himself.

"All right," she said softly.

Quinn lifted her hand to his lips, pressing a hard, thankful kiss into her palm before letting it go. Then he looked down at the man between them.

"It's up to you," he said. "I think I can get your foot out, but there's no guarantee. If I try, it could just mean prolonging the suffering without anything to show for it. And even if I do get it out, there's still no guarantee you won't lose it, anyway. If you'd rather not try, tell me now and Hana will take it off."

"Try," the man said.

Quinn nodded and turned back to the pipe. Wrapping one hand around it, he placed the other flat against the uneven wall and began, very slowly, to pull it all the way out. More grit and dust fell, but nothing more ominous. The pipe was longer than he needed when he finally got it out of the wall—awkward but usable. He maneuvered around the trapped man, squeezing Hana close to the sloping wall, and placed the end of the pipe against the small space between the collapsed ceiling and the floor. Then, bit by bit, centimeter by slow centimeter, he forced it into the crack between the two slabs of concrete. When it was far enough in, he wedged the biggest chunk of concrete he could find under it. Then, rising up as high as he could in the claustrophobic confines of the small space, he braced both hands on top of the pipe and put his back into it.

"Wrap your hands around his knee and get

ready to pull when I say pull," he ordered Hana. "I don't know how high I can get it, or for how long. Fractions of inches, and seconds, is all I can promise."

Hana wrapped her hands around Ross Beecham's knee.

"Ready?"

"Yes," she said clearly. "Ready."

Quinn took a deep breath and pushed. And then pushed some more. He turned red in the face and sweat popped out on his upper lip and across his forehead. And he pushed harder, using his shoulders and his back and his strong, warrior's heart. Metal squealed in protest and the mountain of rubble above them groaned. And still Quinn pushed.

For a long, breathless, agonizing moment, Hana thought nothing was going to happen. And then, suddenly, the ceiling slab moved. Just a tiny inch, a mere nothing of space, but it moved.

"Now!" Quinn said between clenched teeth.

Hana pulled with all her might but it looked as if a mere nothing of space wasn't going to be enough.

"I can't," she moaned.

"Yes, you can. Pull!" Quinn panted, bearing down harder on the pipe. He could feel it beginning to bend under the strain. "Don't worry about hurting him. *Pull!*"

Hana threw herself backward with every last ounce of strength in her. The man's foot came free, and Hana went with it, landing in a heap on his chest with enough force to knock the wind out of him. Her hard hat went rolling into the wall.

Quinn let go of the pipe, throwing himself over Hana to protect her from the recoil as it sprang free. Liberated from Quinn's weight, it snapped up with tremendous force, clanging off the tunnel's ceiling, and then ricocheted off the wall. The noise, as loud as it was, was drowned out under the reverberating roar of the ceiling slab as it struck the floor.

They all three froze for a long, agonizing second—the injured man, supine on the uneven floor; Hana sprawled over him; and Quinn, curled over them both, sheltering them with his big body. The seconds stretched into an endless infinity as the terrible sound echoed through the rubble surrounding them. And then, suddenly, it was quiet. Deathly quiet. And another, more ominous sound, a faint trembling vibration that she could feel through her skin, began to shake the unsteady walls around them.

Quinn was up and yanking on Hana before the change in sound could be registered or cataloged—except that he already had. He'd heard it before. "Move!" he yelled, all but picking Hana up and throwing her toward the tunnel opening. "Get going. Now!"

"But my patient— My bag— You—"

"I'll take care of him. Get moving! I said *move*," he roared when Hana grabbed one of Ross Beecham's limp arms.

"I'm not leaving you here."

"You're not leaving me anywhere. I'll be right behind you. *Move!*"

And Hana moved, scrambling on all fours, scraping her hands and knees on the rough, uneven floor, banging her head on the ceiling when she raised it too high. She crouched lower, falling to her stomach, and kept crawling. The air was thick with dust and grit, making it hard to see, and she could feel larger and larger rocks and chunks of debris hitting her on the back as, one by one, the supporting timbers shoring up the tunnel gave out. Blood roared in her ears, louder than the roaring, creaking mass all around her. Hot tears stung her eyes and flowed, unheeded, down her dirty cheeks.

Because of her, Quinn was in this hellhole. Because of her, he'd put himself at risk. Because of her, he might be trapped again. And this time, he might die. Because, this time, there weren't any professionals to dig him out. *He* was the only heavy-rescue specialist on Paradise and, because of her, he was inside, where he couldn't do anyone any good. Least of all himself.

"Mike," she sobbed, guilt-ridden and panic-stricken, more afraid of him dying alone than dying with him. "Mike." She reversed direction without turning around and began to scramble backward. No matter what he said, she couldn't leave him. "Mike."

Her progress was stopped by something solid.

"*Mike!*" she screamed, thinking debris had already blocked his way and he was trapped. "*Mike!*"

"Dammit, Hana, I said move!"

The something solid was the Mighty Quinn.

Hana changed direction again, still sobbing, tears of joy mixed in with her tears of fright. *He was right behind her.*

She could hear him breathing now, his breath coming in short, rasping, labored pants. He was grunting, too, almost rhythmically. And there was a scraping sound, just barely audible beneath the rumble of the collapsing tunnel. Scrape, grunt, thud. Scrape, grunt, thud. She realized he was dragging the dead weight of the injured man, using the strength of his long legs to propel them both backward along the length of the tunnel.

Hana kept crawling, focusing on the sound of her lover's tortured breathing like an exhausted swimmer focusing on land on the horizon, telling herself that it was going to be all right, that they were going to make it. That they had to make it.

But where in God's name was the mouth of the tunnel?

It hadn't seemed this long on the way in. She should be seeing light by now, the blessed white light of a sunny day; but ahead was only darkness.

Had the tunnel collapsed at the entrance, too? Were they destined to crawl all this way and still not make it?

And, then, suddenly, there it was. The faint white glow of daylight filtering through the dust-laden air of the collapsing tunnel.

"I see it," she said. "Oh, God, I see light. We're almost there." She reached back, grabbing at Quinn's shirt to pull him along with her as she scrambled toward safety. "Come on, hurry. We're almost there. Hurry."

And then she felt a hand on her arm, and then another, and she was being pulled forward, out of the darkness and away from Quinn. She struggled with her rescuers, trying desperately to keep a hand on Quinn's shirt. It ripped, coming away in her hand, and she came tumbling into the light.

"Mike. Mike's still in there," she said piteously, grabbing at the hands that pulled her to her feet despite her wild struggles.

"We'll get him, Hana," Bennie said. "It's all right. We'll get him. But you have to get out of the way."

She moved away from the mouth of the tunnel then, half scrambling away from, half clinging to the hands that held her, her eyes glued to the rapidly crumbling entrance.

And then Big Louie reached in and hooked his hands under Quinn's arms, pulling him the last few feet to safety. They fell backward on the rubble—Big Louie and Quinn and Ross Beecham—like children on a sled with their arms around each other's chests and their legs stretched out in front. Several men rushed in to lift the injured man, unconscious now and totally limp, from Quinn's lap to rush him to the waiting helicopter. Before anyone else could move, Hana launched herself forward and took his place.

"Didn't I tell you you don't always have to be the hero?" she screeched. "Didn't I? But do you listen?" She was sobbing now, tears streaming down her cheeks, and flailing at his chest with both hands. "Do you ever listen? You could have been trapped in there. Or killed. And it would have been all my fault. All my—"

"Hana. Hana, honey, calm down," Quinn said, grabbing at her hands to still her. "It's not your fault. We're all right, baby. Everything's all right now." He clamped both her hands to his chest with one of his and grabbed her chin with the other one, forcing her to look at him. "Hana, it's over," he said, staring into her eyes. "We're safe."

She stilled. "Safe?" she asked, as if she couldn't believe it. "Safe?"

"That's right. We're safe. Everybody's safe now."

She stayed as she was for a moment longer, her body strung tight, her emotions strung even tighter, staring into the eyes of the man she loved. "Safe?" she asked again.

"Yes."

"Oh, God. Oh, God." She flung herself against his chest in an agony of relief and thanksgiving. "I thought I'd lost you."

His arms went tight around her. His eyes closed. "Me, too," he murmured into her hair. "Me, too."

"You've got to promise me you'll never do anything like this again," Hana said into his neck.

He hugged her tighter.

"Mike?" She pushed herself a little away from him so she could see his face. "I mean it. You've got to promise me."

"How can I make a promise like that, Hana? How do I know what's going to—"

"You've got to promise me."

"Promise her," Big Louie said from beneath them, "and then get off me. You weigh a ton!"

HE STRIPPED HER the minute they were behind closed doors, so intent on inspecting her body for cuts and contusions that he ignored her protest that she was all right.

"You're not all right," he insisted. "You've got a big ugly bruise below your left shoulder blade. Here," he said, touching it gently. "And another one just above the right cheek of your rear end."

"Must have been all that falling rock in the tunnel," Hana said, amazed that she hadn't felt it hit her. She still didn't feel it, though she knew she would later. "You could try the leeches," she suggested.

"Ugh, no." He still couldn't believe she'd actually put leeches on his face. "That's disgusting."

"Sissy," she scoffed, but he wasn't listening.

"And look at your hands," he muttered, gently turning them over by the wrists so he could inspect her palms. "Scratched all over. They're a mess."

"They're not a mess," Hana objected. "They're a little scraped up is all. I've had cat scratches that looked worse than that."

"And your knees. Look at your poor knees."

Hana glanced down. "I look like I went skateboarding without kneepads."

"You look like you've been through a war. They need to be bandaged." He backed her up, pressing on her shoulders to sit her down on the closed lid of the toilet, then turned and yanked open the door of the tall metal supply cabinet. "Where's the antiseptic?"

"I could use a little soap and water first," Hana countered, and stood. "And so could you. Mike—" She put her hand on his arm, stopping him from doing further damage to the meticulous order of her supply cupboard. "Let's wash some of this dirt off and *then* we'll see what needs bandaging. Come on," she urged when he hesitated. "Let's take a nice hot shower. We'll both feel better."

"You're right," Quinn agreed. "We need to get the dirt out of those scratches." He turned from the cabinet, leaving it open, and pushed back the shower curtain.

Hana shut the cupboard door and then stood back, letting Quinn fiddle with the water pressure and temperature to his heart's content. "Okay, get in," he ordered when he had it adjusted to his liking.

"You, too."

"Yes, me too," he agreed, stripping off his clothes. "I'm going to wash you."

And wash her he did. He soaped her hands first, holding them between his, rubbing his thumbs gently over her palms and sliding his fingers between hers to make sure they were squeaky clean. Hana tried not to flinch, but the soap and water stung.

"I know," he soothed, holding on to her hands so she couldn't pull them away. "But it'll only hurt for a second."

"That's what I tell my patients, too."

He grinned at that. "And they don't believe it, either, I'll bet."

"Not for a minute."

"Well, be a brave little soldier," he advised. "It'll be over soon." He squatted down to give the same gentle treatment to her scraped knees.

Hana looked down at the top of his bent head, and abruptly found herself blinking back tears. Not since her mother had died, almost twelve years ago, had anyone treated her with such loving tenderness. She was always the one looking out for the welfare of others. It was…nice, she thought; really quite incredibly nice to have someone take care of her for a change. She lifted her hand to his hair, threading her fingers through the thick, water-slicked strands, and encountered a lump the size of a walnut on the side of his head.

"Why didn't you tell me you were hurt?" Hana demanded, running quick, skillful fingers over the rest of his head.

He tried to duck away from her touch. "It's nothing."

"Head wounds are not 'nothing.'" She put her other hand on the opposite side of his head to hold him still while she finished probing. "Are you having any blurred vision? Dizziness?" She cupped his chin and turned his face up to hers. "How many fingers am I holding up?"

"Three," he said, and reached up to take them in his hand. "Hana, I'm fine."

"Are you?" Her other hand was still cupped under his chin. His hand was on her thigh. Her look was serious and intent. "Are you really?" she asked, meaning more than just physically.

"Yes. I'm fine. Really."

Their gazes locked, loving and anxious. And suddenly, it was all too much. The reality of what had almost happened hit them both at once.

"Hana," he said and rose to his feet. "Oh, Hana." His arms went around her in a death grip, locking her body to him as if he would never let her go.

Her arms were no less tight around him. "Mike," she breathed, and lifted her mouth to his.

The kiss was fierce and wild, an affirmation of life, a tempestuous celebration of their narrow escape from death and danger. Their tongues thrust and parried in a heated explosion of raw passion, teeth nibbling and biting, heads twisting to find a better position until, finally, he grabbed a handful of her hair and pulled her head back, holding her still for his tongue's invasion. She moaned and gave him what he wanted, opening her mouth to his tongue the way she longed to open her body to his complete possession. She slid her hands, fingers spread wide, down the sleek, water-slicked muscles of his back to his tight masculine buttocks, and pressed him to her, her nails adding emphasis to her erotic demand. He thrust forward, grinding his erection against the soft skin of her stomach.

"Please," she sobbed, arching against him in carnal entreaty. The ache was unbearable. "Please. I need you inside me. Now."

"Yes. Oh, God, *yes.*" He released his hold on her hair, dropping his hands to her buttocks to lift her to him. She wrapped her legs around his waist. "Now," he groaned and thrust himself into her welcoming heat.

Her back slammed against the cool tiles of the shower stall with enough force to jar her teeth, but her only response was to tighten her grip around him and demand more. "Harder," she moaned into his neck. "Please, Mike. Harder."

And Quinn thrust harder, his feet braced wide on the textured floor of the shower, his teeth bared, his whole body straining, his muscles bunched and tight, burning, as he strove to give them what they both so desperately desired.

It claimed them in a glorious burst of white-hot passion that sent them hurtling through inner space and seemed to last forever. Hana's delicate tremors escalated into shudders, and then to violent, uncontrollable shock waves that sent Quinn reeling into passionate delirium right alongside her.

Her chest was heaving when the shock waves finally passed, and she clung to him, her face buried in the hot skin of his neck as she gasped for air to fill her lungs. But he drove her up again, before she could catch her breath, sending her higher, faster, with a force that shook her to her soul. And again. And again. And again, until she was begging him to stop—the same way she had begged him to take her.

"I'm sorry," he said into her neck. "I'm sorry." He couldn't remember ever needing her so much as he did then. Wanting her so badly. But he'd almost lost her and, despite the long, intense kisses and the soul-deep closeness and the driving, relentless passion that kept him pounding at her, he still couldn't quite believe she was all right.

"I'm sorry," he said again, trying to discipline the raging desire that threatened to overpower them both.

He loosened his hold on her, letting her slide down his body until her feet touched the floor of the shower stall. She leaned into him weakly, her thighs trembling, her insides still quivering from the wondrous, torturous, glorious heights he'd driven her to.

"I didn't mean to hurt you," he said, stricken by her utter defenselessness and his own callous disregard of her vulnerability. Here she was, already shaken by her brush with death, and he had taken her without finesse or tenderness, leaving her shivering and weak, trembling against him like a kitten who'd been hit. He felt like a beast. "Hana, sweetheart, I'm so sorry."

"Don't be silly," she said, still panting into his chest. "You didn't hurt me." She looked up so he could see her face, knowing she must look like a woman who'd been deliciously, exquisitely and very thoroughly loved. "You...overwhelmed me," she said, deciding that that about explained it. "But you most certainly didn't hurt me." Her lips curved up in a smile that was satisfied femininity incarnate. "And if you'll give me a minute to catch my breath, I'll be happy to have you overwhelm me again."

"Are you sure?"

"What? That I loved being overwhelmed by you, or that I wouldn't mind being overwhelmed again?"

"That you're not hurt?"

"Do I look hurt?"

He had to smile at that. Standing there, looking up at him with her lips rosy and kiss-swollen, her face flushed and glowing, her body wet and naked and utterly luscious, she looked like a debauched wanton. He reached to put his arms around her again.

She placed her hand against his chest. "Let's finish our shower and get out of here before we turn into a couple of prunes," she suggested, her eyes hot as she looked up at him. "Then you can take me to bed."

Still looking at him, her eyes full of passionate promise, she lifted her hands and began to unbraid her hair. Quinn reached out to help her, and what was supposed to be a hurried cleansing became a slow feast for the senses. They soaped each other slowly, thoroughly, with exquisite attention to detail, searching out tender spots to soothe and murmur over and kiss away the hurt. Soft hands smoothed over a hard, hair-roughened chest and swelling biceps; callused palms massaged the slender curve of a waist and the delicate flare of hips; lips brushed shoulders and fingertips, the tender roundness of a cheek and the chiseled plane of a jaw. They washed each other's hair, and each other's back and each other's feet. And then, finally, they turned the water off and dried each other with the same tender care. Quinn sat on the toilet seat while Hana toweled his hair dry and he returned the favor, using a blow dryer and brush on her long black hair until it rippled down her bare back like fine hot silk. They conscientiously applied antiseptic to each other's wounds and then he picked her up and carried her to bed.

There, the loving was tender and prolonged, sweet, hot and life-affirming. And full of lovers' promises.

"I'll make you so happy," Quinn swore, whispering the pledge against the tender skin of Hana's breast.

"I'll never leave you," he vowed, stroking his

hands down the quivering skin of her stomach. "Never."

"I'll love you forever," he promised, the words soft and warm against her ear as he entered her body. "Till death do us part and beyond."

But he didn't promise never to put himself in danger again. He couldn't.

"I've just got myself back, Hana," he said when they lay together in the aftermath of passion. "All of me. And I can do my job again. I'm not saying I'll never be afraid." He rolled up on his elbow so he could look down at her. "Hell, I was afraid today. Scared to death," he admitted freely, without the shame that saying it would have caused him less than twenty-four hours before. "You know it and I know it and everyone on Paradise knows it. But my fear didn't stop me this time. Thank God," he added fervently. "And now I know it will never stop me again." He brushed the tumbled hair away from her face with the backs of his fingers, smoothing it out against the pillow. "And it's all because of you, Hana," he said softly. "You gave me back my manhood."

"No. No, I didn't. Because you never lost it. You only mis—"

Quinn turned his hand and cupped her cheek. "You gave it back to me," he said and pressed his thumb against her lips when she would have resumed her protest. He looked into her eyes, a small, wistful smile playing around the corners of his mouth. "You're not going to ask me to give it back, are you?"

There was only one answer she could give to that. Only one thing a loving woman could say to a man like Mike Quinn. "No." She turned her lips into his palm. "No, I won't ask that. Ever."

"Oh, Hana. Hana." He lowered his mouth to hers, slowly, lifting her into his kiss with the hand on her cheek. "I love you," he murmured. "More than you'll ever know."

"Not more than I know," Hana said against his lips. "Not more than I love you."

Quinn sighed and laid his head on her breast, feeling mightier than he ever had in his life.

a machine like Chang? No." She turned her lips
into his palm. "No, I won't ask that. Ever."

"Oh, Hana, love." He lowered his mouth to
hers, slowly, deliberately, sealing his with the hand
on her cheek. "I love you," he murmured. "More
than you'll ever know."

Epilogue

THE WEDDING WAS HELD two weeks later, as
planned, on the white sand beach behind Hana's
clinic.

The bride wore a traditional *paréo*, a length of
silky fabric knotted above her breasts—vivid yellow flowers splashed across a white background—glorious against her tanned skin. Her
black hair flowed over her shoulders and down
her back, held off her face by a fragrant crown of
island blossoms that matched the bouquet in her
hands.

The groom was all in white. White duck pants
with a white dress shirt, unadorned except for the
impressive physique it covered and the flower lei
around his neck, made for him that morning by
his bride.

Like all the wedding guests, both bride and
groom were barefoot.

The ceremony was short and sweet, presided
over by a local cleric and Big Louie, who, as a full-
blooded Polynesian, felt eminently qualified to
bless them in the name of the ancient island gods.

They exchanged simple bands of gold, as precious and enduring as their love for each other,
and sealed their vows with the traditional kiss at
the ceremony's end. And then Hana offered her
bridal bouquet to the sea, flinging it past the foam-

ing waves to invoke a life of happiness for them on Paradise.

They feasted on roast pig supplied by Bennie Chu's Beachside Bar and Grill, and mountains of side dishes and fruit salads and pies prepared in a dozen different ways by the local women. The island council presented them with a draft for the new legislation regarding island building codes—and Quinn, with one full-time job as Paradise's new—and first—fire chief. The grateful hotel developers presented an enormous bank draft to cover the cost of replacing the contents of Hana's lost medical bag, and then some. And a grateful Ross Beecham—who wasn't going to lose his foot, after all—sent a crate of live lobsters, a case of French champagne and his undying thanks.

"It was perfect, wasn't it?" Quinn said with satisfaction as they lay face-to-face in the hammock, long after the last of the wedding guests had finally gone home. He was naked except for a simple gold band on the ring finger of his left hand and the crown of flowers that had somehow been transferred from Hana's head to his.

Hana was equally attired in nothing but a gold wedding band, except for the silky veil of her hair and the strong arms of her husband around her. "Perfect," she agreed, snuggling deeper into Quinn's embrace. She smiled into the warmth of his neck. "Though I can think of one thing that would make it even better."

"I thought we already did that." She could hear the satisfaction and pleasure in his voice. "Twice."

"Not *that*," Hana said, chuckling. "Although it was very nice. Both times." She tilted her head back against Quinn's arm, shifting position slightly so she could look up at him. "I haven't given you your wedding present yet."

His smile was warm and loving. "I thought you were it."

"Not all of it."

"Not all of it? You mean you've got other ways to drive me crazy?"

"No." She took his hand and pushed it down her body to her stomach. "I mean, the rest of it's in there."

"The rest of—?" She watched, pleased, as realization and joy came together in his face. He stroked her stomach with gentle fingers. "You mean a baby?"

"I mean a baby," she said.

"When?"

"That night in the water. After we delivered Darlene Kapaua's little girl."

"The very first time we tried?"

"The very first time," she confirmed.

A grin split the Mighty Quinn's face. "Damn, I'm good," he said.

Harlequin Romance®

Delightful

Affectionate

Romantic

Emotional

Tender

Original

Daring

Riveting

Enchanting

Adventurous

Moving

**Harlequin Romance—the
series that has it all!**

HROM-G

HARLEQUIN PRESENTS®

HARLEQUIN PRESENTS
men you won't be able to resist
falling in love with…

HARLEQUIN PRESENTS
women who have feelings
just like your own…

HARLEQUIN PRESENTS
powerful passion in
exotic international settings…

HARLEQUIN PRESENTS
intense, dramatic stories that will keep you
turning to the very last page…

HARLEQUIN PRESENTS
The world's bestselling romance series!

Harlequin®
Historical

From rugged lawmen and
valiant knights to defiant heiresses
and spirited frontierswomen,
Harlequin Historicals will
capture your imagination with
their dramatic scope, passion
and adventure.

Harlequin Historicals...
they're too good to miss!

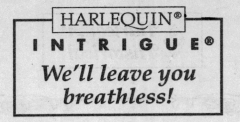

LOOK FOR OUR FOUR FABULOUS MEN!

Each month some of today's bestselling authors bring
four new fabulous men to Harlequin American Romance.
Whether they're rebel ranchers, millionaire power brokers
or sexy single dads, they're all gallant princes—and
they're all ready to sweep you into lighthearted fantasies
and contemporary fairy tales where anything is possible
and where all your dreams come true!

You don't even have to make a wish...
Harlequin American Romance will grant your every desire!

Look for Harlequin American Romance
wherever Harlequin books are sold!